IT DIDN'T HAPPEN

Other titles by Sandra Glover

IT DIDN'T HAPPEN

SANDRA GLOVER

Andersen Press • London

First published in 2005 by
Andersen Press Limited,
20 Vauxhall Bridge Road, London SW1V 2SA
www.andersenpress.co.uk

British Library Cataloguing in Publication Data available
ISBN 1 84270 077 4

Typeset by FiSH Books, London WC1
Printed and bound in Great Britain by Bookmarque Ltd.,
Croydon, Surrey

Chapter 1

Laura woke from a restless half sleep and glanced at the display on the alarm clock as the doorbell rang. 02:34. Thursday morning already, her mind registered as her feet swung over the side of the bed.

She'd been quick to move. Very quick. But her parents had been quicker. Laura could hear the stamp of their feet, the incessant ringing of the bell and, from along the corridor, the sound of Jenna crying.

Laura wanted to follow her parents downstairs. This could be news. At this time in the morning, with the rain beating down outside, what else could it be? What else but the terrible news they'd been expecting for the last four days?

But outside her bedroom, she hesitated. It wouldn't be fair to leave Jenna, alone in her room, crying. Jenna was only six. Hearing the doorbell in the middle of the night, she wouldn't know what to do. So Laura headed for her sister's room, switched on the light, sat on the end of the bed and hugged her.

'It's all right,' Laura said. 'Sssh, it's all right.'

A lie, of course. Nothing was right anymore. How could it be, with Paul gone? They'd tried to shield Jenna from the worst of it but she wasn't stupid. Yesterday she'd asked Mum if Paul had gone to be with Jesus and Mum had nodded, before collapsing in tears.

'Sssh,' Laura said again, as Jenna's howls grew louder. 'It'll be. . .'

The sound of the door opening. The sound of her mother's scream, freezing the words in Laura's throat.

Grabbing Jenna's hand, Laura rushed to the top of the stairs. Saw the strange tableau in the hallway. Her dad leaning against the now closed door. His face white. His features fixed in rigid shock. Her mother, no longing screaming, but sobbing. Clutching someone, holding him close.

Paul.

The someone was Paul.

Laura's mind went immediately into denial, her body into slow motion, as she made her way downstairs, still holding Jenna's hand.

This wasn't her brother. It couldn't be Paul. Paul was dead.

This wasn't even happening. It was a cruel dream. The same dream she'd had for three nights now. The dream where Paul came back. Where she touched him, held him, spoke with him.

Yet, somehow, this wasn't like the other dreams. In the other dreams, Paul had been Paul. Looking exactly the same as he always did.

Not like this. Bare-footed. Wet. Dripping. Soaked through. Mumbling to himself and rocking in Mum's arms. Water dripping onto the hall carpet, as if Mum was, somehow, squeezing him dry with her embrace.

2

Jenna was pressed close to Laura. She'd stopped crying but Laura could feel the beat of Jenna's heart, the movement of her chest, as though she was screaming inside.

'Is it a ghost?' whispered Jenna, her voice trembling with genuine fear.

Ghost he might be, for all Laura knew. He was pale enough. But solid. Definitely solid. Surely of this world?

As she reached the bottom stair, Laura could hear Paul's mumbled words. The same words repeated over and over, in the same monotone.

'It didn't happen. It didn't happen. It didn't happen.'

She wanted to go to Paul. Touch him. Hold him. But she couldn't. Mum was still clutching him like a tigress fiercely guarding her cub.

'Get a blanket. Get some dry clothes,' Mum screamed at Laura.

'I'll phone an ambulance,' said Dad. 'We need to get him to hospital.'

Her dad's words were spoken calmly, practically. All the emotions you might expect, in these circumstances, strangely absent. Absent from Laura too. As if her mind had decided it couldn't cope with confusion, shock, panic, terror and delight all at once, so had simply decided not to feel anything at all.

Police, Laura thought, as she made her way back upstairs to find the blanket and clothes. They'd need to inform the police. How urgent was it? How soon did they need to know?

Over the past few days, as the evidence that Paul had

3

drowned slowly turned from dreadful possibility to almost certain, Laura had imagined all sorts of scenarios ... The police coming to break the news that Paul's body had been washed up somewhere along the coast. The final proof ... Or, more likely, Paul's body never being found. The eternal hopelessness.

Nothing had prepared her for this. Paul coming back alive had been her hope, her prayer but not something she could actually allow herself to believe. Yet here he was.

'You can carry some of the clothes,' she told Jenna.

It was the kindest way to stop Jenna's sharp little nails digging into Laura's hand. Give her something to do. Make her feel useful. Make her concentrate on getting downstairs with a bundle in her arms.

In the kitchen, Dad pacing, the phone to his ear. Mum drying Paul's hair with a towel. Not easy with Paul rocking on his chair, still chanting those words.

'It didn't happen. It didn't happen.'

As Mum started to get Paul changed, Laura noticed the scratch marks down Paul's left arm, the slight bruising around his shoulder, as though someone had been gripping him tightly. But otherwise he didn't look too bad for someone returning from the dead.

Returning from the dead. She shuddered, dismissing the idea. Paul wasn't dead. Hadn't ever been dead. It had all been a terrible mistake. Whatever they had thought, whatever the police had led them to believe, was wrong. So, if Paul hadn't been swept out to sea and drowned what HAD happened last Saturday night? And where on earth had Paul been for four days?

Paul was clearly in no position to tell them. Mum was talking to him. Sobbing words of comfort. Asking questions. Getting no response, except for those same words, repeated at intervals.

'It didn't happen.'

Shortly before 3am, the doorbell again. This time the ambulance. Hurried negotiations. Laura volunteering to stay home. To put Jenna back to bed.

Laura wasn't sure Jenna had ever been fully awake, even when she'd walked downstairs with the bundle of clothes in her arms. Certainly she'd drifted back into deep sleep the minute Laura had laid her in the bed.

Laura waited a few minutes, just to make sure, before returning to the kitchen, to make herself some coffee. What else was there to do?

'You're sure you'll be all right?' Dad had said. 'I'll phone as soon as we get there.'

Before they even arrived, by the sound of it. The phone was already ringing. Were you allowed to use mobiles in an ambulance?

'Hello,' Laura said, not bothering with name or number, feeling certain it was her dad.

'It's Detective Inspector Fallows. Is that Mrs Crompton?'

'No. It's Laura.'

'Laura, are your parents there? I had a message that

your father phoned. I'm not sure it's been passed on right, though.'

'I think it has,' said Laura. 'It's Paul. He's come back.'

Momentary silence.

'Are you sure?'

Laura nodded at the phone.

'Sorry,' came the policeman's voice, repeating the question. 'But are you sure? Can you tell me what happened?'

Laura explained. Feeling it all slipping out. Confused and disjointed. How could it be otherwise?

'And the girl? What about Melissa? Was she with him?'

Melissa. The word was like an electric shock. Sharp. Painful. Jolting Laura into the guilty realisation that, in the turmoil of Paul's return, she'd barely given Melissa a thought.

'No. I told you. He was on his own. Just Paul.'

'And he didn't mention her?'

'No. He didn't say anything. Just those same words, over and over . . . "It didn't happen."'

'Are you on your own?'

The words less brisk now, more of the human being, less of the cop.

'With Jenna.'

'I'll send a WPC round.'

'No, I'm fine.'

'She's a trained counsellor. You might need someone. Jenna might.'

No point arguing. He was trying to be kind. And the last words had convinced her. Laura was close to Jenna.

She'd been thirteen when Jenna was born. Ten-year-old Paul had been moody, jealous of the infant intruder. He'd barely acknowledged Jenna for the first three years of her life. But Laura had been as besotted about baby Jenna, as she'd once been about baby Paul. Only by the time Jenna arrived, Laura was old enough to be useful. Volunteering to babysit, to wheel Jenna round the park, shovel food into her dribbling mouth, bath her, play with her, change smelly nappies. Anything.

Anything but try to explain, six years on, about Paul. It had been left to Dad to tell her why Paul had gone to heaven to be with Jesus. And Laura didn't fancy trying to explain why Jesus had, apparently, sent Paul back. If Jenna, woke, hysterical, confused, screaming about ghosts, it might be handy to have a trained counsellor around.

Laura sat down and stirred her coffee, twirling the spoon round and round, creating dark stormy waves. Seeing in them two figures battling for their lives. Two teenagers allegedly swept out to sea. Paul and Melissa.

But, clearly, it hadn't happened that way. Paul was back. So wasn't it likely that Melissa was back too? Ought she to phone Melissa's parents?

No. Contact was best left to the police. If Melissa was back, all well and good. If she wasn't, it would be too easy to raise false hopes with the news of Paul's return. To say the wrong thing. To set them off screaming hysterical abuse down the phone again. To make matters worse.

Not that things could be much worse for Melissa's parents. And, regardless of how abusive they'd been over the past few days, somewhere in the midst of her own pain, Laura had summoned enough compassion to feel sorry for them.

Melissa was their only child. Spoilt, pampered, doted on, adored. Beautiful and clever. Destined for a brilliant future. Until double tragedy struck. The first dreadful blow six months ago and now her disappearance. Were the two related? Had Melissa been desperate enough to try something stupid? Had she, somehow, persuaded Paul to help her?

Questions. Always questions. Never any answers.

Laura abandoned the coffee and paced up and down, trying not to speculate too much. What was the point? They'd been over all the possibilities so many times over the past four days. Four agonising days that felt more like four months, four years, four centuries.

She stared at the phone, willing it to ring. But when it did, the news was disappointing.

Paul was restless, feverish. The doctor had seen him. Would see him again later in the morning. The police had arrived, anxious to speak to Paul about Melissa, who still hadn't turned up. But the doctor wouldn't let them. It wouldn't do any good anyway. Paul hadn't said anything. Only those words.

Dad had offered to come home but Laura had persuaded him he'd be better staying with Mum, with Paul. Luckily the WPC had arrived in the middle of the phone call, convincing Dad that she and Jenna were in safe hands.

There were no formalities.

'I'm Fran,' the female officer had said, accepting a cup of coffee. 'How's the little one?'

'Still asleep,' said Laura.

'You might want to get some rest, yourself, now I'm here.'

Laura had nodded.

Resting would be better than talking. Lying on the settee, closing your eyes, trying not to think, letting your subconscious take control. Hoping your dulled mind would somehow sort it all out for itself. Hoping that the morning might bring real answers from Paul himself.

What had happened to Paul and Melissa last Saturday night? Where had Paul been for four long days? And where was Melissa, now?

Chapter 2

Sitting by the bedside of the sleeping Paul, on Thursday afternoon, Laura watched constantly for signs of change. She'd barely eaten since Saturday night when Paul had failed to return home. Any sleep she'd managed to get had been disturbed and disjointed but strangely, she felt no tiredness. In fact she felt full of energy, alert, hyper-active almost.

It was hard to sit still. That morning she had busied herself getting Jenna ready for school. It would be best, the WPC had advised, for Jenna's routines to be kept as normal as possible and Jenna had run off into the playground, quite happily, it seemed. Accepting, at face value, the good news that Paul was back. But was he?

Looking at him now, it was hard to be sure. His face was incredibly pale, framed by the light brown hair which flopped untidily across his forehead. Under the thin covers, Laura could see the outline of his limbs held rigid. No peaceful, relaxed sleep this. More like deep shock. Or worse, the stillness of death itself.

Suddenly Paul sat up. One fluid movement. No previous stirring, no warning. Laura screamed but Paul seemed not to hear her or even be aware of her presence, though his eyes flicked rapidly, unnaturally, around every centimetre of the room.

'Paul?'

'It didn't happen,' he shouted out.

'Paul, it's me, Laura.'

'It didn't happen,' he repeated more flatly, mechanically.

Laura tried a reassuring sort of smile and gently touched Paul's hand but she resisted the temptation to speak again. It was as her parents had warned her. The response to every word, phrase or sentence spoken was the same. Like the time Jenna's 'Talking Ted' had got stuck and all the little bear had said for weeks was 'Ted wants to play'. Eventually Dad had cracked, taken it to pieces, ruined it completely and rushed out to buy another in the hope that Jenna wouldn't notice the difference.

The trouble was, you couldn't simply buy another Paul. If the doctors managed to take him to pieces, as it were, what guarantee was there that they could put him back together again?

Laura pressed the bell to summon the nurse, as she'd been told to do if there was any change. Paul followed her action with his eyes, then looked at her face with some sort of recognition.

'Hi,' she said, forgetting her resolution not to speak.

The programmed response came almost before the short word was out of her mouth.

'It didn't happen.'

'OK, sweetheart,' said the nurse who had just come in. 'Nice to see you back with us again. Now let's have a feel of your pulse and check your temperature.'

Laura waited for Paul's refrain but nothing came. Was that because the nurse's voice was unfamiliar or was it the way she seemed to speak to the room in general rather than to Paul in particular?

'Perhaps you could open the blinds now.'

Again the comment seemed to be addressed to the room but Laura guessed the nurse meant her and was pleased with the excuse to stand up, stretch her legs, have a prowl round, while the nurse attended to Paul.

From the third-storey hospital window, Laura could see out across the houses, right down to the coast where the sea glistened blue and calm. Deceiving you into believing it was harmless. Hiding its secrets.

'That might be a bit too bright for him,' came the nurse's voice, as Laura finished opening the blinds. 'Perhaps we could have them half open.'

Laura adjusted the blinds, blocking out some of the bright, January sun. The weather had changed again. No longer raining but cold and crisp, as though it might be about to snow. Laura shook her head, marvelling as she'd done so many times over the past few days, how ordinary, mundane thoughts could still intrude with all manner of trauma and chaos going on around you. The weather, for goodness' sake! How could she be thinking about the weather, with her brother lying there, nursing an empty shell where his brain used to be?

A pretty smart brain it had been, too. Not that Paul always used it. Especially where the dreadful Melissa was concerned. But he'd always done well enough at school.

Better than Laura, anyway. She always had to do tons of work for fairly mediocre results, while Paul sailed along, effortlessly, getting top marks.

It was happening again! Ordinary thoughts, petty jealousies, creeping in, as though everything was fine. As if she didn't have anything more serious to think about than the unfairness of their respective school grades!

'That's good,' said the nurse. 'Temperature's normal. And the pulse.'

'But he's not talking,' Laura hissed. 'I don't think he even knows where he is. Or who he is!'

'Hard to say,' said the nurse. 'Doctor should be in to look at him again soon. Are your parents around, by the way? Doctor will want to speak to them.'

'They should be back any minute,' said Laura, looking at her watch. 'Dad's popped home to collect some of Paul's things and I sent Mum to get herself a cup of tea.'

As the nurse left, Laura sat down by the bedside again. Paul was lying back but his head was propped up on the pillow and his dark brown eyes were open and active. Very active. Flickering like the digital eyes of a robot, in one of the sci-fi films Paul was so fond of, engaged in working out how many seconds there are in 300,000 light years.

Only Paul didn't come up with any smart answers. Laura leant forward, trying to attract his attention, trying to get him to focus. She pulled a silly face at him. No response.

'It looks like it might snow,' she said, sitting back and

13

trying to casually address the room as the nurse had done. 'Jenna'll be pleased. She was dying for it to snow all over Christmas, remember? So she could use that sledge you and me bought her. But it didn't. Christmas! Seems ages ago. But it isn't. Schools have only been back two weeks and I was due to start back at college on Monday, wasn't I? Only I never went. Because you didn't come home on Saturday night. And they found your jacket and trainers washed up on the beach. And they said…and we thought…Paul, can you hear me? Can you see me? Do you understand what I'm saying? We thought you were dead, Paul. We thought you were dead!'

'It didn't…'

'Don't,' said Laura, bursting into tears and rushing from the room. 'Don't. I can't bear to hear you say that again.'

Laura's parents sat with Paul for the rest of the day. Laura couldn't face going back. She volunteered to pick Jenna up from school. Took her for some fish and chips and then straight on to her ballet lesson. Getting her changed, lacing up her ballet shoes, admiring Jenna's concentration as she did her exercises at the barre. Wishing that her own concentration was half as good. Wishing she could stop her mind wandering back to that hospital room. Seeing Paul, lying there, calling out those words.

She'd been in contact with her parents through the late afternoon and early evening. There'd been no real change, they said. He'd had some dinner. Been sick. Drunk a lot of water. Kept it down. Even managed a bit

14

of dry toast later. So that was good news, wasn't it? And no, he wasn't talking at all. Just those same three words.

'You weren't watching my dance!' Jenna complained, as the class finished.

'Yes I was,' said Laura, vaguely remembering twenty pink-clad girls flitting round the room, furiously flapping their arms. 'You were a lovely butterfly.'

'Robin,' said Jenna, petulantly. 'I was being a robin.'

The plan was for Laura to take Jenna straight home after the ballet but she didn't. Instead of phoning her parents for a final check-in call, she drove straight to the hospital, overwhelmed by a sudden feeling of optimism.

She was right. When she arrived, Paul was sitting up in bed, looking normal enough for Jenna to be allowed a quick peep before Dad drove her home.

A camp bed had been set up in the small room so that Mum could stay the night and Laura volunteered to sit with Paul while her Mum went for a shower.

'There's been a big improvement tonight,' her mother whispered as she picked up her towel and toiletry bag. 'He's starting to recognise us, I'm sure he is. I mean, it's weird, like most of his mind's somewhere else but he grabbed hold of my hand earlier and stared at me, like he wanted to say something.'

'And?' Laura prompted.

'He said those same words,' her mother admitted. 'But I don't think he meant to. I'm sure he was trying to say something else. Whatever's going on in his head, he's fighting it. He's coming back to us. I know he is.'

15

'And what do the doctors say?'

'Nothing much but they've done some tests and they'll do some more tomorrow, when he's a bit stronger. Hopefully, he'll be talking by then...'

'And there hasn't been any news about Melissa?'

'No. Nothing. But the police have been to see her parents. I'm afraid Paul's return has set them off again ... you know.'

Laura nodded. Her mother didn't need to explain further. The Kingsley–Porters had been so adamant, so certain. Telling the police and anyone else who would listen that whatever had happened on Saturday night, Paul was to blame.

'Look,' said her mother, suddenly, looking over in the direction of the bed. 'He's sitting up. I think he's trying to say something.'

'He's pointing at the glass,' said Laura. 'I think he wants a drink.'

'Or maybe he wants to get up,' said her mother, walking across. 'No, Laura, come here! I'm sure he's trying to say something.'

Chapter 3

PAUL

I wish they wouldn't do that. I wish they wouldn't talk about me as if I'm not here. But I don't suppose I can really blame them. They can't see what's going on in my mind, can they? And I can't tell them. I can't even show them by a nod or shake of my head. Because every time I try to answer, say something, do something, I start feeling sick, panicky and this huge iceberg appears in my head, freezing my mind, leaving me gibbering those words I don't mean to say.

I've just done it again and they looked so hurt. So disappointed. Mum shaking her head as she wandered off for her shower, Laura standing with her back to me, so I don't see the tears. But I know they're there.

So, OK. I guess the trick is to stay quiet for a while. Try to get a grip. Think it out rationally. Practise talking in the safety of my own head. Try to unfreeze the iceberg.

It's not that I can't remember things. I can. At least some things. It's definitely starting to come back but I can't get it to make sense. It's all mixed up. Like someone's cut up a magazine and pasted it in my head. A crazy collage of pictures, stories, words and colours. Lots of colours. And, if that wasn't bad enough, I'm peering at it through that block of ice so it's all sort of hazy, distorted, images constantly changing, like a kaleidoscope. But I've got to sort it out, somehow.

It's funny because distant memories are the easiest. Like it's supposed to be for old people. Can't tell you what they had for dinner but they'll give you the names and life histories of every kid they were at school with. Maybe it's deliberate. Maybe that's where they'd rather be. Back in the past with their youth, their health, their fun. Maybe they don't want the present with its creaking bones, wrinkled skin, incontinence and fears of death. Maybe I don't want the present either.

Because the most recent memories, the ones I know are important, won't come. And when I try, the closest I can get is about a year and a half ago. Something that happened then.

Something I'd rather forget but I know I shouldn't. Because, somehow, I know it's the starting point.

It was a Thursday morning, only three days into the new term at the start of Year 10 and I was doing my new paper round. It was raining. No big deal considering I live on the north-west coast but dark, cold, miserable and wet enough to make me wonder why I'd thought a paper round was such a good idea in the first place.

Money was the prime motivator, I guess. It always is with me. Mum says I'm a compulsive spender which is strange because the rest of the family are dead tight. Laura's got a few thousand in the bank already. All her Saturday and holiday job money goes in there. Birthday and Christmas money. Everything. Just so she can sit gloating over her bank statement every month. And Jenna's nearly as bad. Six money boxes she's got. I can see them all lined up on her windowsill. So that's good, isn't it? I can remember some ordinary, everyday things like Jenna's money boxes. All six! The pig for pound coins, the cat for 50p pieces and so on.

But me. I can't save at all. I just can't resist the latest CD, video game or sci-fi book. Not to mention my fatal attraction to Crunchies and Mars Bars. So the money from my paper round came in handy.

Then there was the added bonus. I was the new boy, only joining the team in the middle of August, so I didn't get the cushy town runs. I got the country route, delivering to the hamlets and isolated farms along the narrow lanes. Generally deserted between six and seven in the mornings except that sometimes, on fine days, the wonderful, brilliant, fantastic, funny, delicious, mega-gorgeous Melissa Kingsley-Porter would be out riding her horse.

Melissa. Why does the name hurt so much, now? It didn't hurt back then. I'm sure of that.

Sometimes I'd see her from a distance, cantering round the paddock at the back of her house or trotting along the side of the river. Sometimes she'd be right there on the lane and I'd squeeze my bike into the hedge to let her pass. Trying not to gawp. Trying to think of something sensible or witty to say.

'Hi,' was the best I ever managed.

If any conversation took place, it was Melissa who

started it, while I tried to control the blush which spread from my toes, right to the roots of my hair.

And this with a girl I'd known since infants! Who was in my tutor group at school. In most of my subject sets. I wasn't even that interested in girls back then but I made an exception for Melissa. Everybody did. She was an exceptional sort of person.

It wasn't only her looks . . . though long blonde hair, enormous, bright blue eyes, perfect skin, slim figure and sensationally long legs do tend to get you noticed a bit in our dull little town . . . it was her confidence. The way she was always there, bubbling, fizzing and gushing at the centre of everything. She was nice too. The sort of person who could transform your day, just by smiling at you.

Oh, I know Laura wouldn't agree. She's always had a real downer on Melissa, has Laura. Ever since infants when I used to come home crying every day because Melissa had called me 'Spot' again or refused to hold my hand in circle games, screaming that she didn't want to catch that horrible disease.

The 'disease' she was so scared of was my eczema. Not a disease at all, in fact, and certainly not contagious. Just an unsightly, irritating skin condition. But Melissa wasn't to know that, at the time. We were only five, for goodness' sake, and there were plenty of other kids who didn't fancy holding my rough, raw hands or who screwed up their flawless little faces at the red blotches on my cheeks and dry scabs under my ears.

They all got used to it after a while though, and the

teasing died down. In fact it was Melissa who put a stop to it once and for all when we were in top juniors. We'd been playing rounders and Jimmy Beckett started yelling at me because I'd dropped an easy catch.

'Leave him alone,' Melissa said, coming up and holding one of my hands in hers. 'Look at this? How do you expect him to catch with his hands all bleeding? It's not his fault he's got eczema, is it? Come on, Paul, let's go and get your cream.'

Of course, Laura had only sneered when I'd told her.

'Teacher watching, at the time, was she?' Laura said.

Well, OK, yes. Miss Halliday had happened to see and I heard her congratulate Melissa later for being so kind. And maybe it was no coincidence that Melissa nabbed 'The Kind and Helpful' award, again, at the end of that term. But it didn't matter. That wasn't the point. Melissa had spoken, so all the other kids obeyed. The eczema wasn't my fault. It was OK to touch my hands.

And, since that time, Melissa had always been dead thoughtful about my eczema.

'Tell Mr Addis you're not doing cross country today,' she'd say. 'It'll only set your skin off, running about in the rain.'

Or,

'Look at that crack in your finger. I don't know how you can hold your pen with it like that. Shall I get you a plaster?'

'Patronising cow,' Laura had once said, when she'd heard Melissa advising me to get contact lenses because my glasses were rubbing red blotches under my eyes and round my ears.

But Melissa was right. And that was another reason I'd taken on the paper round. I'd decided to try to save up a bit of money for some lenses. Mum wouldn't buy them for me. Said they'd be more trouble than they were worth. That I'd be forever losing them. But she couldn't stop me if it was my own money, could she?

Laura had laughed and said it was because of Melissa. But it wasn't. I wasn't that much of an idiot. I knew there was no way Melissa would fancy me with or without specs. I'd just got fed up with them rubbing my skin and they could be a real nuisance. Especially in the rain.

That particular morning was a good example. After I'd shoved the last paper through the last letter box, I put my head down and tried to cycle home as quickly as I could. No point hanging around. You wouldn't have caught Melissa out in that sort of weather. But I had to keep stopping to wipe the rain off my glasses. And that's when it happened.

I stopped on a bend, took my glasses off, breathed on them, gave them a wipe with a soggy tissue and put them back on again. I didn't set off immediately because of the noise. Above the sound of the lashing rain, I could hear sheep bleating but that's not what bothered me. It was the irritating buzz in my ear, like I'd got a pool of water sloshing around my eardrum. Then, of course, by the time I'd finished rubbing and shaking my ears, my glasses needed wiping again.

As I was on the second wipe, it dawned on me that the buzzing sound wasn't in my ears at all. It was coming from the field on the right. Not a bee sort of buzz. More like the sound of a muted vacuum cleaner, so I guessed the farmer might have some sort of machine going.

A bit pathetic, I know, but I like tractors and stuff, so I rode my bike up the bank a bit and had a peep over the hedge.

Big mistake. Big, big, mistake. Because what I saw was no tractor or muck spreader. It was a spaceship.

Even in the dark and the rain, with my steamed-up glasses and the spiky hedge obscuring my view, I was certain it was a spaceship. I was certain then and I'm certain now. Though I think there was a time in between when I wasn't sure at all.

Isn't it amazing how quickly your brain can process information when it has to? Mine went into overdrive that morning...Dull, greyish metal – yellowish, circular patches on top – flattish, triangular – fins jutting out – a bit like a plaice on a fishmonger's slab – but hovering – half a metre from the ground – buzzing – not particularly big – five metres across? Seen something similar before – but only in books – sci-fi books – probably not real – imagination – hallucination – do sheep hallucinate? Huddled at top of field – bleating – watching – they see it – real – spaceship – alien spaceship – oh shit!!

In the quarter of a second it had taken for the information to scurry round my brain a dozen times, I was down that bank, skidding onto the lane and pedalling off

23

round the corner. Only there was a kid standing right in the way. Throwing its long, thin arms into the air, screaming at me. High-pitched. Not an ordinary scream. Not an ordinary kid. Eyes on top of domed head. No obvious mouth. No nose. Wobbly body. Like dark green blancmange.

Green was the word I focused on as I felt my body and the bike part company. Cursing the fact that I wasn't wearing my helmet as my head slammed onto the lane. But it was the sharp pain in my arm that made me pass out, I reckon. Because I was conscious for a moment when I fell. I know that, because at the same moment that the pain raced from my wrist to the top of my shoulder, I saw the legs. Just legs. No feet. Rubbery, spindly legs. Green legs.

Whether it was the fall or the shock or the pain or all three, it took a good few minutes for me to come round. And a few minutes more before I dared open my eyes. I had to open and close them several times before anything came into focus at all and even then it was all sort of blurry. But there were no legs. No funny green kid.

I stood up, rubbed my head, stretched my arm, wriggled my fingers. Amazed that I could stretch and wriggle at all, that nothing was broken. Once I'd realised my arms were working, I tried to rub a bit of the mud off my clothes. Don't ask me why. Dirty clothes should have been the least of my problems. But I did all the rubbing and cleaning before I wandered back up the bank and peered over the hedge again.

Nothing. The sheep were still huddled at the top of the

field but they'd stopped bleating and, apart from them, the field was empty. No spaceship. Just a triangular patch of shrivelled grass.

The rain had eased off too and it seemed sort of lighter. I began to panic that I'd been unconscious for longer than I thought, but no. My watch said 7:04. The usual sort of time I'd be on my way back. Just in time to have breakfast, get changed and catch the 8:15 school bus.

It took me a bit longer than usual to get home though, because I had to push the bike. The wheel had buckled and besides, I still couldn't see too well. Funnily enough, I didn't bother to check whether my glasses were broken, probably because my mind was full of other things. Like seeing a spaceship and a little green alien standing in the lane.

Only I hadn't really seen them, had I? The fall from the bike had obviously come first and the alien encounter after, as the result of a bump on the head. Because aliens didn't really exist, did they? And people who claimed to have seen them were nutters, weren't they? And I wasn't a nutter, thank you very much. Therefore I couldn't have seen them. Could I?

I was still going through this self-brainwashing routine when I turned into our road and heard the shout.

'Paul! Are you all right? What's happened? Where've you been? I've been frantic.'

And there was this fuzzy red figure coming towards me. I took my glasses off and the fuzzy red thing transformed into my mum in one of her posh work suits.

'Look at the state of you! You've had an accident.'

'I fell off my bike,' I managed to say. 'It's OK. It's no big deal.'

'No big deal!' she said. 'Paul, do you know what time it is? You've missed your bus, Laura's had to take Jenna to nursery and I'm going to be late for work. And I've been worried sick! I tried your mobile and it rang on the hall table, where you'd left it . . .'

'But . . . but . . .'

I looked at my watch, mid-stammer, and began to guess what the fuss might be about. It still said 7:04.

'Er,' I said lamely. 'I think I might have knocked myself out, when I fell off. What time is it, exactly?'

'It's twenty-five past eight. And what do you mean, knocked yourself out? You mean you lost consciousness? I've told you time and time again to wear your helmet. Come on, we'll phone school and then I'm taking you to the doctor.'

I tried to tell her I was fine and naturally I didn't mention anything about spaceships or little green men. I mean she was flapping enough as it was. Absolutely insisted on the doctor and, if I'd told her about the other stuff, it would have been a psychologist or a full brain scan at the very least.

It was on the way to the surgery that I noticed something a bit odd. I could see the road signs. Not only see them, I could read them, clearly. And my glasses were still in my pocket. Only when I tried them on again, did my vision go blurry.

When I mentioned it to the doctor, he tutted a bit, shone a light in my eyes and recommended that Mum took me up to Casualty for an X-ray. But before he let me go, he ran his fingers around my face and examined my hands.

'Your eczema's cleared up, Paul,' he said. 'Told you it might, as you got older.'

Mum and I looked at each other. My eczema had been driving me nuts with its itching and bleeding for weeks. Only that morning I'd woken up with the usual mess of flaky skin and bloodstains on the sheet. But the doctor was right. My hands weren't blotchy red anymore. They didn't even feel particularly rough. And the cracks in my fingers which had plagued me while I was posting newspapers had completely healed up.

I looked at the doctor. Looked at my smooth hands. Saw both, perfectly clearly without my glasses. And that's when I started to have my first really crazy thoughts. That's when everything started to go wrong.

Chapter 4

Her mother was taking a long time in the shower, Laura thought, and Paul was getting restless. Sitting up. Lying down again. Eyes shut. Eyes open. But even when they were open, he didn't seem to be seeing her or anything else in the room. As if the eyes were focused on some distant place or time.

At least, Laura hoped they were. Because she preferred the thought that his mind was somewhere, rather than nowhere at all. If it was somewhere, then there was a chance they would get Paul back. If not...

She shook her head, denying the possibility that Paul would spend the rest of his life in some sort of vegetative state. There had to be brain activity, didn't there? He was moving. Laura was no medical expert but she knew that every blink, every twitch of the fingers, all the little movements we usually take for granted, don't just happen on their own. They require some sort of brain connection.

Sitting down, on the edge of the bed again, she took Paul's hand in hers. It was sticky, clammy but the skin was soft and smooth. Miraculous proof of the body and mind's ability to heal themselves, given the right... or wrong... circumstances.

The eczema, which had plagued Paul for the first

fourteen years of his life, had suddenly disappeared following a minor cycling accident. The same accident which had somehow corrected Paul's vision.

'See,' Paul had said. 'All those years of skin creams, pills and special diets were a waste of time. You should just have hit me over the head with a blunt object!'

Doctors had been mystified. But the biggest mystery, Laura felt, was not the improvement itself but the impact it had.

She and her parents had spent years telling Paul that physical appearance didn't matter. That it was what was inside that counted. That people would love you for what you were, not how you looked.

Wrong, it seemed. Within a month of the eczema's disappearance Paul had acquired a whole new set of friends and his very first girlfriend, Ellie. Was it because Paul suddenly felt more confident, more normal, Laura had wondered, or were people really so stupid? Didn't they know that Paul had always been attractive, caring, intelligent and funny? Had they really only ever seen the blotches and sores?

'It didn't happen,' Paul suddenly screamed out, his hand tightening around Laura's.

He was staring at her, shaking his head, moving his lips but nothing else came out and he lay back on the pillow, exhausted, eyes closed again.

Laura touched his face. Was losing the eczema quite the blessing it had first seemed, though? Strange to imagine but if he'd still had the skin defect, then he probably

29

wouldn't be lying here now, calling out those awful words. Because, with the eczema, there's no way Melissa Kingsley-Porter would have latched onto him.

In some ways, Laura was surprised that Melissa had showed interest in Paul at all. Boys her own age were hardly Melissa's style but then, she was the sort of person who could never resist what someone else had got. If someone had a new, trendy jacket, then Melissa rushed out and bought a more expensive version. Whatever the current fashion was, in clothes, hairstyles, games machines, Melissa had to have the biggest and the best.

So once Melissa had seen that other girls were interested in Paul, it was only a matter of time before she gave it a try, staked her claim. Snatching him, literally, from under Ellie's nose. Just to prove she could.

Laura knew all the gory details because it had happened at Paul's fifteenth birthday party. Paul had never wanted parties as a kid. Parties, to Paul, were places where you had to watch other people stuffing their faces with things you weren't allowed to eat and sit out of the circle games when no one wanted to hold your hand. His birthdays had usually been celebrated by taking a couple of carefully selected friends to the cinema.

So, when Paul had announced that he wanted a fifteenth birthday party, Mum and Dad hadn't liked to refuse. On the other hand, they were full of the usual parental angst about inviting thirty, probably drunken, teenagers, to rampage around the house till the early hours of the morning.

Should they stay in and keep an eye on things?

'No way!' Paul had yelled.

In the end, they'd compromised. Mum, Dad and Jenna would spend the night at Gran's and Laura would stay home to keep a semi grown-up and civilised eye on the party. With strict instructions to phone Mum, if too many windows got broken, if the kitchen became too awash with vomit or if the neighbours threatened to call the police about the noise.

Not a role Laura had particularly relished, though the party had been a quiet enough, not to say fairly dull, affair until Melissa arrived, very late, wearing a dress you could have caught a chill in at midday in the Sahara, let alone on a November night on the west coast.

Not hard to tell Melissa wanted to be an actress, Laura had thought. It was like she was practising for the Oscars already. Full war paint. Wide, toothy, predatory smile. Looking at least two years older than everyone else, including Laura herself.

Paul and Ellie were smooching, somewhat tipsily, to a disco which had been set up in the conservatory, when Melissa finally quit posing in the doorway and strolled up to them.

'Happy birthday,' Melissa had said, edging Ellie away and slipping a slim, beautifully wrapped present into Paul's pocket.

'Probably a packet of condoms,' one of Paul's mates hissed, as Melissa's arms went round Paul's neck and her lips fastened on his.

'It's only a birthday kiss,' said Laura, trying to restrain a tearful and angry Ellie. 'Come and have a drink.'

Probably a mistake. By the time Ellie had gulped a tumbler full of wine, Paul and Melissa had disappeared and a now more than tipsy Ellie went staggering round the house trying to find them.

'They're in Paul's bedroom!' Ellie announced, lurching back into the kitchen. 'And the door's locked!'

'Er, not a good idea, Ellie,' Laura had said, as Ellie opened one of the drawers and pulled out a vegetable knife.

'I'll kill her,' Ellie screamed.

'Not with that,' Laura had said, taking the knife from her. 'It can barely negotiate carrot peel, let alone Melissa's thick skin.'

When Melissa finally emerged from the bedroom, tugging at her dress, so it almost covered her backside, Laura had considered offering Ellie the services of a rather more substantial carving knife. She'd thought better of it, partly because blood stains would have made such a nasty mess on the carpet and because Ellie was, by that time, curled up fast asleep in the up-turned laundry basket.

Laura and Paul had cleared up all the spilt beer, trodden in crisps and other debris by the time their parents returned the next day. The only mess Laura hadn't been able to deal with was Melissa.

Part of Laura knew that she shouldn't interfere at all. Paul was growing up. He didn't need, and certainly didn't want, her protection anymore. So, apart from hinting that he'd been less than fair in his treatment of Ellie, she'd kept her mouth shut and hoped that Melissa would be satisfied with the initial conquest and leave Paul for the less mature, less sophisticated girls.

Sadly, it hadn't happened quite that way. Paul was immediately and utterly besotted. Spending the best part of that day on the phone to Melissa. Arranging to meet her that night. Coming home dejected when Melissa failed to turn up. Euphoric the next day when Melissa apologised for missing their date . . . she'd had to get the vet out to her horse.

For a rather large and robust–looking beast, Melissa's horse sure got sick a lot. Not to mention the sudden visits she had to pay to her aunt in Manchester, the endless nights she had to babysit for her neighbour or the number of young male 'cousins' she was seen in town with.

But, between excuses, she'd turn up at the house, smiling and gushing, making a big fuss of Jenna and even bigger fuss of Paul until even Mum and Dad were taken in.

'Such a lovely girl, Melissa! And so mature. You'd never think she was only fifteen. Don't you think Paul's matured a lot since he's been seeing Melissa, Laura? So much more confident.'

And so it had gone on. Melissa turning up on Boxing Day with expensive presents for all the family. Melissa inviting Paul to a party on New Year's Eve, only to have to cancel because her fairy godmother had arrived unexpectedly from Outer Mongolia, or something like that. Laura couldn't really remember. Melissa had fobbed

Paul off with so many bizarre excuses during the few months they were allegedly going out together. And he couldn't see. He just couldn't see how she was playing with him!

A sudden groan, from Paul, drew Laura's attention back to him. His eyes were open, staring towards the door. Laura turned to look, expecting to see her mother or a nurse. There was no one, yet Paul was getting more and more restless. Pulling himself up into a sitting position, still staring at the door, rocking from side to side.

As Laura wondered whether she ought to press the bell, she heard shouts and the sound of heavy footsteps scurrying around. Sounded like they had some sort of emergency going on out there.

She gently pressed Paul's shoulders, urging him to lie down, trying to calm him herself. It seemed to be working. As the activity outside subsided, so did Paul's restlessness and he lay back again, eyes closed, exhausted.

'Sorry I've been such a long time,' said Laura's mum, suddenly reappearing, looking as pale as the white dressing gown she was wearing.

'Mum, what is it?' said Laura, getting up. 'What's happened?'

'Melissa's parents,' her mother hissed, dragging Laura to one side, as Paul let out another low moan.

'Have they found her?' Laura asked. 'Have they found Melissa?'

'No, nothing like that,' her mother said. 'They just came to talk, that's all.'

'At this time of night?' said Laura, looking at her watch.

'What does time matter?' said her mother. 'I doubt whether they knew if it was day or night.'

'So what did they want?' Laura asked. 'What did they say?'

'It started off calmly enough,' said her mother. 'Asking how Paul was. How we were bearing up. And I thought for a minute, just for a brief moment, that they were genuinely concerned. But then, it all started to come out. How the police had told them the basics. How Paul was obviously in some sort of denial. How it proved what they'd being saying all along. And they really believe it, Laura. They really believe Paul's harmed Melissa, in some way.'

'It's not possible,' said Laura, looking over at her brother, who was rolling his head from side to side, but was otherwise still.

No one who knew Paul could believe him capable of harming anyone. Or anything.

'I know it's not possible,' said her mother. 'And I think the police do too. But try telling that to Melissa's parents. Before I knew what was happening, Mr Kingsley-Porter was yelling in my face. Telling me that everyone in town knows Paul's a nutter. Delusional, he called him. Mentally unbalanced. And, all the time, his wife was screaming that she blamed herself. That she should never have let Melissa get mixed up with Paul again. I'm surprised you didn't hear.'

'I heard something,' said Laura. 'And I think Paul did too. There was a lot of scuffling and shouting...'

'They had to call security,' said her mother. 'To get Melissa's parents out.'

'It's not Paul who's mad or delusional,' Laura snapped. 'It's them.'

'Please don't say that,' said her mother. 'It doesn't help to start hurling insults.'

'It helps me,' Laura hissed. 'Honestly, all that stuff about Paul being a nutter. They seem to have forgotten, it was their bloody daughter who started the stupid business in the first place! Spreading those pathetic stories.'

'Keep your voice down,' said her mother. 'Paul might hear you.'

Chapter 5

PAUL

Laura's wrong about Melissa. Whatever happened, whatever it is I'm trying to remember, it wasn't Melissa's fault. None of it was her fault.

Oh, Mum and Laura aren't even sure I recognise them but I do. It's just that maybe I'm not showing it too well. Like my facial expressions are as frozen as most of my brain. And they think I can't hear them, whispering, over in the corner. But I can. I've heard a lot of things over the past two years, which I wasn't supposed to. My hearing's always been good but after my 'close encounter', it got a whole lot better, along with the vision and the skin. Only the hearing wasn't something people would notice, so I kept the improvement to myself.

I kept the spaceship and the alien on the lane to myself too. I mean, I wasn't going to damage my new found normality, no way! Having ditched the eczema and thick specs, I wasn't going to set myself up as a different sort of social pariah, was I? The loony who sees little green men!

In a way, it was easier to believe I'd imagined it all. That, at best, it was the result of the bump on the head, when I fell off my bike. I mean, I'd always been a bit of a science fiction freak. I'd watched the films, read the books, played the games, even worn the T-shirts, when I was a kid. And, I'd once read somewhere, that believing in aliens was the first sure step towards seeing them. So hallucination seemed the most likely explanation and, believe me, it was a whole lot better than accepting it was true. That I really had been buzzed!

So, on Friday morning, the day after my little accident, when I'd convinced Mum I was well enough to do my paper round, I tried my best to believe the men I found examining the field.

They'd set up a tent, right in the corner, where I'd seen the spaceship. And when I stopped to ask what they were doing, they said they were from DEFRA investigating a fungal infestation.

Not many people use that lane and those that did, including the farmer who owned the field, didn't seem to think it strange that the men were there for weeks, doing their tests. Nor the fact that when they left, nothing ever grew in that corner of the field again. Not so much as a blade of grass.

And, of course, nobody, except me, connected the goings-on in that field with the story that appeared in the local, weekly newspaper on that same Friday morning. Page 4. Full spread. An article on the strange lights and triangular-shaped object which had been seen hovering out to sea. Witnessed by several different people, at several different times, over the previous week.

Everyone at school thought it was hysterical. It didn't

help that one of the witnesses was 'Cider Joe', well-known local vagrant and wino. Another was Lucille Meredrith, otherwise known as Loopy Lu – an ageing, bike-riding, vegan eco-warrior who rattles tins down the precinct, on behalf of Greenpeace and the Anti-Capitalist League.

Well, I wasn't going to ally myself with those two, was I? Or even with the two or three slightly more respectable witnesses.

'Oh yes, what you saw was probably the spaceship that landed in the field. I met the pilot. Bit green and hysterical but seemed a nice little chap . . .'

So I pushed it all to the back of my mind, where I guessed it belonged. Only it wasn't that easy. The day after the paper came out, I had the first of the dreams and the minute I woke up, I started drawing.

And that was the beginning of my double life. On the surface, everything was great. For the first time in my life, I started to enjoy school. Not the lessons, I hasten to add. Lessons were pretty much as they'd always been. I'd never been what you'd call a swot but, then again, I'd never had any trouble with work either. It sort of came easy to me and I could potter along getting decent enough grades without too much effort.

No, it was the other stuff that changed. It didn't take people long to notice the new me.

'You look different, Paul,' someone said, on the morning after my 'accident'. 'Hey, have you got lenses?'

'No,' I muttered. 'I've had this new laser treatment.'

Well, they weren't to know, were they? And it was

better than trying to explain how my vision had, miraculously, corrected itself.

'And your face doesn't seem so...'

It was Ellie who'd spoken and I could see her, blushing furiously, searching for the right word.

'Er...blotchy,' she finished, lamely.

'New tablets,' I said. 'I don't know whether they'll clear my skin up permanently. The eczema might come back when I've finished the course.'

I added that bit, to sort of cover myself. I couldn't convince myself that the eczema had gone for good. That I could wear shorts for games, instead of hiding my sores beneath baggy, cotton jogging bottoms. That I could go swimming. Go bowling and actually bowl without fear of the balls carving gashes into my fingers.

It was at the bowling alley, about three weeks later, that I got my very first snog. My eczema might have gone but my bowling was still useless. Like my football, cricket, tennis, swimming and athletics. And for the same reason. I hadn't had much practice. Too many years spent hanging round watching, smothering myself in useless creams.

'Oh, Paul!' Ellie had said, after I'd followed the ball halfway down the lane. 'You are sweet!'

And she dragged me back, put her arms round my neck and started kissing me, while everyone cheered and hooted so much that the whole lot of us nearly got thrown out.

I wasn't really sure I wanted a girlfriend. I hadn't thought much about girls. Except Melissa, of course. And, to be honest, that's why I lapped up the attentions of Ellie and the others. In the hope that Melissa would notice. That she'd start to wonder what she was missing.

Year 10 boys weren't really Melissa's style. I'd only ever known her to go out with sixth formers or college boys. But, eventually, she made an exception for me. Said I was mature. Not like the other nerds in our class. That she'd always known I was sort of special.

Yeah, I know Laura reckons that Melissa was only ever stringing me along. That I treated Ellie like shit...but I didn't. We were only kids. It's not like it was anything heavy. Nothing you could really call a relationship. And like I was supposed to turn Melissa down just because I'd been seeing Ellie for a few weeks. Oh sure!

Every lad in our school wanted to date Melissa. Except perhaps Patrick Greenway who campaigned for 'The Gay Rights' party in our mock elections! Even the Year 7s used to hang around the stairs to the maths rooms hoping to get a look up Melissa's short skirt. Dirty little beasts!

So once I started seeing Melissa, that was it. Instant popularity. Instant superstar status. Or as near as you get to being a superstar round here. And that part, the surface part of my life, was great. Unbelievably, fantastically-better-than-life-had-ever-been sort of great.

And, for months, I managed to ignore the other part. Or, at least, stop it intruding. Nights and early mornings were the worst. The dreams.

I didn't get them all the time. Maybe only one a fortnight, at first. Then, by Christmas, two a week.

Increasing to three, then four. And, by early spring, I was having them almost every night.

I say them. But it was really the same dream, over and over, accompanied by its own weird soundtrack. And the minute I woke up, I'd start drawing. I couldn't help it. The compulsion to draw completely took over. And if I fought it, if I managed to leave the house, I'd find myself stopping, halfway round the paper run, to draw on the newspapers I was supposed to be delivering.

Naturally, I lost the job. Partly for being late all the time and partly for defacing papers. Defacing was a bit of a cheek. The drawings were well good. I've still got piles of them tucked away in the drawer under my bed.

Funnily enough, they didn't seem to have anything to do with the dreams. Not at the time. They were all seascapes. Some fairly normal-looking scenes with hammer-head sharks, jellyfish, and electric eels. Others featured whole undersea cities with coral towers and transparent domes. And the wildlife in those scenes bore no resemblance at all to anything you'd see on a David Attenborough documentary. The only thing all the drawings had in common, was that they all featured an octopus somewhere. Like I was being dead pretentious, using a trademark!

I took to scribbling the drawings everywhere. On the backs of envelopes or my shirt sleeves. On the serviettes when we took Mum to 'The Blue Boar' for her birthday. On my exercise books at school.

Most of the teachers weren't too pleased about that but

Mr Forrest, the art teacher, picked up my Geography folder, when I was in the library one lunchtime, catching up on a bit of coursework.

'I didn't know you could draw like that, Paul,' he said. 'How come you didn't take art?'

Because I can't draw, was the simple answer. Because my people still look like balloons on stilts and my cars like hunchbacked slugs on wheels. All I can draw is seascapes.

'They'd look great in water colour,' he said. 'Pop into the art room, sometime. Give it a go.'

Which is how I came to have my paintings displayed in the prime spot in the school foyer.

Nobody commented much, except to say they were good. No one thought it was particularly odd, at the time. Why should they? They didn't know the other weird things that were going on in my head, did they? They didn't know I'd started to put two and two together and come up with an answer that certainly wasn't four.

Part of me still wanted to ignore it all. But it was getting harder. I'd wake from the dreams, in the early hours, start drawing, stagger into school shattered, and, by mid-afternoon, I'd be falling asleep over my maths.

So I decided to test my crazy theory. Running up a massive bill on the Internet. Checking up on people who'd had similar experiences. There were thousands of them. Literally thousands! And they were only the ones who wanted to share their experiences. Who's to say there weren't thousands more out there, like me, who just wanted to hide it and make it go away?

The best tip I got from the Net was also the worst.

'Dreams are common,' one of the sites informed me. 'But if you're troubled by them, talk about it. Once you get it out in the open, you'll find the dreams will start to fade.'

Well, OK, maybe I should have got it out my system, safely, anonymously, on the Net. But I didn't.

The day after reading the advice, me and Melissa were eating lunch, out on the school field. It was late May. Just before or after half term. I can't remember now. But it was warm enough to sit outside. Warm enough to make me feel sleepy.

'What's with you, these days?' said Melissa, dripping 'Highland Spring' bottled water onto my face. 'You're always asleep.'

'I'm not sleeping too well at night,' I confessed. 'I keep getting this recurring dream.'

'Is it about this gorgeous blonde, who's trying to seduce you?' she said, dangling blonde hair in my eyes as she leant to kiss me.

'No, I think I could handle that,' I said. 'Trouble with this dream is that I don't really know what it's about. I just get this feeling... of being paralysed. Like there's a single massive weight pressing down on me. I can't move. I can't speak. And my head seems to be swelling with noise.'

'What sort of noise?' said Melissa.

'High-pitched but very musical. Beautiful almost. But it sort of takes over my mind and I don't want it there.

All I want to do is shake my head, cover my ears with my hands but I can't move. And the funny thing is, that even when I wake up, I can't move. Not for five minutes or so. Sometimes more.'

Melissa looked at me, sort of seriously.

'I think I've read something about this,' she said.

I wondered, for a moment, if she'd been on the same websites I'd been visiting.

'It's called sleep paralysis, I think,' she said. 'People get it sometimes if they've got some major trauma going on in their lives. Bereavement, divorce, redundancy, that sort of stuff. But you haven't, have you? I mean everything's OK at home, isn't it?'

'Sure,' I said. 'No probs.'

'Hey, this isn't about us, is it? You don't feel trapped by the relationship, do you?'

Trust Melissa to make it personal!

'No, the dreams started way before we were going out. They started after . . .'

The bike accident. That's what I should have said. Let Melissa think a nasty bump on the head had caused the dreams. Let her think I needed nothing more than a good neurosurgeon.

Instead I paused. Looked at her.

'Listen,' I said. 'If I tell you something, promise you won't laugh. Promise you won't think I'm nuts.'

'Paul, I know you're nuts! That's why I love you! Nothing you could say could possibly make any difference.'

Love. She actually used the word love. I know she

didn't mean it. I knew at the time. But I guess it made me feel sort of happy, sort of secure.

So I told her about seeing the spaceship and the little green man, with the wobbly body and wavy arms. Melissa's lips started to twitch, at first, until she realised I was serious.

'And you think,' she said, 'that your dreams stem from that? From seeing your alien?'

'I think it's worse than that,' I confessed. 'I've been looking on these websites, see? Alien sightings are dead common. There's a lot more than you'd think. People see them all the time. All over the world.'

'Sure.'

That single word, the tone, should have warned me but, by then, I was too anxious to spill it all out.

'But the people who just see the spaceships or aliens don't usually get the dreams or do the drawings...'

'So you reckon your paintings are tied up with this too, are they?'

'I know they are! And my eczema clearing up and my 20:20 vision. The thing is, Melissa, I don't just think I saw an alien. I think I was abducted. I think I must have spent some time on that spaceship. I think they must have operated on me. I don't actually remember any of it but...'

Melissa lifted her hand, like she wanted to stop me but I was well into it all by then.

'I mean, I know it sounds mad, but it's got all the classic features. The time lapse. My watch stopping. The physical changes. The dreams. The music. The drawings.

46

And it's not just me. You should see all the websites. All the people who claim to have had exactly the same or very similar experiences.'

'Yes,' said Melissa. 'But most of them are in mental homes. With people who think they're God or Elvis. Why are you telling me all this, Paul?'

'I don't know,' I said lamely. 'Talking about it is supposed to help clear your head. Get rid of the dreams and stuff.'

'Yeah but I think you're supposed to talk to a counsellor, Paul. Or a shrink or something,' she said, getting up.

'I'm sorry,' I said. 'I'm probably just imagining it. Getting worked up about Mocks. It's just stress, that's all. Look, don't tell anyone, will you?'

She gave me a withering look.

'Like I'm going to admit I'm going out with an A-class loony?'

But she smiled when she said it, grabbed my hand and told me to get a move on 'cos the bell had just gone. So I guessed she'd just forget it.

And I still don't honestly think she meant to tell. That's just Melissa for you. Opening mouth before engaging brain. Blurting things out. Anything to attract an audience. And once she'd got one, it was in her nature to exaggerate, dramatise. Not that she needed to exaggerate much. I'd given her everything, hadn't I?

Within days, the story was all round the school, spinning out of control.

'Hey, Paul, seen any little green men lately?'

'What's it like on Planet Ga–Ga, Paul?'

'Reckon your alien pals could pay me a visit? I need some help with my art coursework.'

I backtracked, of course. Tried to deny it. Said I'd just been having a joke with Melissa. But people wouldn't let it drop.

'When's your next space-trip, Paul?'

'How's the X-ray vision? Can you see my undies?'

'Eczema cured by aliens . . . you could sell that to *The News of the World*!'

Well, Melissa wasn't going to go out with an object of fun, was she? So I got dumped. And I couldn't believe I'd been so stupid. Why had I told her? I was mega depressed for weeks, missing Melissa, missing the street-cred she gave me, cursing myself for having been such a prat.

There was a bright side though. The dreams stopped and, when I tried to draw, my sharks turned out like squashed melons with fins and my jellyfish like deflated parachutes. So, there I was. Back to normal. Social outcast with no friends. Wonderful!

But I didn't blame Melissa. Not about that, anyway. Whatever Laura says, I know Melissa didn't do it on purpose. She didn't do any of it to be cruel. But then something happened. Something happened with Melissa. Something I don't want to think about.

Chapter 6

'Are you crazy?' Laura said to her mother on Friday, as they sat in the hospital café, trying to work up an appetite for the sandwiches, which sat, untouched, in front of them. 'It's too soon. He's not well enough.'

'There's been a big improvement, this morning.'

Oh, massive, Laura wanted to say. Apparently Paul had managed to nod when asked if he'd like some cereal for breakfast. He'd managed to get up, go for a shower, sit in the dayroom for a while. He'd picked up a car magazine while he was there. Seemed to be reading it. Understanding. Only when Mum had asked if he could remember what her car was like, or Dad's, those words had come out.

'It didn't happen.'

And Mum thought he was well enough to face questioning! No ordinary questioning either. They were bringing in a hypnotist.

'Surely,' Laura said, after nibbling a corner of her sandwich, 'they could give it another couple of days? See what sort of progress he makes on his own. You said yourself, he's been nodding and shaking his head, in answer to simple questions.'

'Not the sort of questions the police want answers to,' said her mother.

Laura bit into her sandwich again. The doctor hadn't let the police talk to Paul yet but he'd tried himself. Starting with questions like 'Would you like a drink?' and 'Shall I open the window?' Getting nods in response to both. Gradually building up. Getting on to 'Do you remember going to Melissa's house on Saturday night?'

'It didn't happen,' Paul had screamed out.

Carried on screaming until they gave him a sedative.

'You know what happened when the doctor tried,' said Laura. 'Paul's not ready for those sorts of questions yet.'

'Not on a conscious level,' said her mother. 'That's why they suggested hypnotic regression. It provides a safe environment for him to talk . . .'

'Safe!' said Laura. 'So you think letting some crazy witch-doctor delve around in Paul's mind, digging up whatever trauma might be in there's safe, do you? What about that poor woman we saw on telly the other week? The one who's suing a hypnotist for dragging up memories of child abuse? She hasn't been able to leave her house since!'

'That was a stage hypnotist!' said her mother. 'I'm talking about a trained hypno-therapist. Not someone who's going to mess around in Paul's mind for fun! For entertainment.'

'So what ARE they fishing for?'

'You know that, as well as I do, Laura,' said her mother, wearily. 'If there was just Paul to consider, they'd maybe let him have more time to work it through, himself. But it's Melissa. Her parents are putting a lot of pressure on the police.'

Pressure from the Kingsley-Porters wasn't likely to be

ignored. Melissa's dad was a lawyer. Her mother had been an accountant and town councillor. She'd given both up, after what had happened with Melissa, six months ago, but she still had a lot of contacts. Still knew all the important people.

'And it's in Paul's best interests,' Laura's mother was saying. 'Surely you can see that?'

'No,' said Laura. 'No, I can't. So you'll have to spell it out for me.'

'When Melissa and Paul were both missing,' said her mother slowly, 'I don't think many people believed what the Kingsley-Porters were saying about Paul being responsible. I think they knew, like we did, that it was the grief talking.'

'Good,' said Laura. 'Because, if anything, it would have been the other way round, wouldn't it? Melissa doing the manipulating. Melissa pulling the strings. Like she always did.'

'Or,' said her mother. 'It was all accidental. Nothing sinister. No manipulating. But Paul coming back changes things.'

'Does it?'

'Perhaps not in the essentials, no. But in people's minds, it might. Especially as Paul's in some sort of denial. Melissa's parents are making a big thing of that.'

'I know that!' Laura snapped. 'It doesn't make them right.'

'So the sooner we can get Paul talking, the better it will be,' her mother insisted. 'At worst it will end all the rumours, all the speculation. At best, he might be able to tell us where Melissa is. The police are optimistic. They think there's a fair chance she's still alive. But she won't be able to last much longer... not on her own. Not in her condition.'

Laura nodded. She might not like the idea of what they were going to do to Paul but her mother was right. They didn't really have a lot of choice.

'I'm going back to the ward,' she said, swallowing the last mouthful of sandwich.

'I won't be long,' said her mother, who'd yet to touch either her sandwich or her cup of tea.

It was strange, thought Laura, as she headed back upstairs, how little we really know about the human mind. The way it reacts to stress. How impossible it is to control sometimes. Since Saturday night, she'd felt no desire to eat, there'd been a constant sickness in her stomach, pains across her shoulders and down her legs. She knew they weren't real, physical pains as such but she couldn't make them go away.

Strangely Paul didn't seem in such bad shape, physically, for someone who'd been missing for four days. So was it, as the police had initially suggested? That Paul and Melissa had simply taken themselves off somewhere? That Melissa had simply needed to get away for a while? But, if so, why had Paul come back alone? Why was he so traumatised?

Laura arrived at the ward, just as Paul was returning from having his lunch in the dayroom with other patients. He walked, unaccompanied, back into his room and settled himself in the armchair, whilst Laura perched on the end of the bed.

'Did you have a nice lunch?' she asked, remembering to use questions which only required a nod or shake of the head.

This time it was a nod, accompanied by a smile, which made her think, for the first time, that Paul really recognised her. That he knew who he was talking to.

'It's Laura,' she said, as casually as she could. 'Remember me?'

Paul raised an eyebrow and rolled his eyes, looking for a moment like the old Paul. Like he might be about to say, ''Course I remember you, stoopid! How could anyone forget your ugly mug? Think I'm crazy or something?'

No words followed the look. But this was definitely progress. Mum had been right. Paul was getting better all the time.

It suddenly occurred to Laura that, though Paul obviously wasn't ready to speak, he could, maybe, write things down. She got a pen out of her bag and picked up one of Paul's Get Well cards. It was from Ellie. News certainly travelled fast in their little town.

'Hi!' Laura wrote on the back. 'How do you feel?'

She gave the card and the pen to Paul.

He gripped the pen, quite normally, naturally. Looked at the message. Looked up at Laura. Let the tip of the pen touch the card.

Maybe not such a good idea, Laura thought, as she saw Paul's expression change to one of panic, frustration and his knuckles whiten as his grip tightened on the pen. He stabbed the pen up and down on the card a couple of times, before bending over to write. Forming his words, slowly, carefully. Taking forever.

Eventually he shoved the card towards her.

'I,' he'd written. 'I . . . I . . . It didn't happen.'

'It's OK,' Laura said, trying to force back tears. 'It's OK.'

She doubted whether he'd heard. He'd slumped back in the chair, eyes closed, as if the effort of writing, or trying not to write those three words, had exhausted him.

Laura stood up, paced about the room, cursing herself for being so stupid. Why had she done that? Why had she put pressure on him? What had made her think that she could succeed where the professionals had failed?

A hand touched her shoulder, as she stood staring out of the window, making her jump.

'Sorry,' whispered her mother. 'I was trying to get your attention, without waking Paul.'

Laura was about to tell her mother what had happened but her mother was still speaking.

'I've just phoned your dad. He's on his way,' she said, looking at her watch. 'Should be here before Paul starts his treatment. He'd have been here earlier but he got a phone call from Melissa's mother and then—'

'She phoned Dad at work?'

How had she been able to track him down, Laura wondered? Dad had only popped into work for a couple of hours to get a few things sorted out.

'Yes,' Laura's mother was saying. 'And you know what a strong voice she's got, at the best of times. Apparently half

54

the office could hear. I think she's really flipped. Lost it completely. Your dad tried to reason with her but it was no good. In the end he had to put the phone down. She phoned back five times before your dad got fed up and told his secretary to say he'd just left.'

'Shouldn't we tell the police?' said Laura. 'Turning up here, last night. Phoning Dad at work. It's harassment, isn't it?'

'Your dad's contacted them already but he doubts they can do anything or even whether they want to. I hope it's just your dad being paranoid, but he seemed to think the police are starting to be convinced by Melissa's parents. They actually asked your dad whether there was any truth in what Mrs Kingsley-Porter said.'

'Which was what, exactly?'

'That Paul hated Melissa,' Laura's mum said, wearily. 'That's what Mrs Kingsley-Porter was screaming down the phone, over and over.'

'Hated her?' said Laura. 'Now I know she's flipped. After everything Paul's done these last few months? How could she possibly say that?'

'She's claiming that was all an act. That Paul actually planned to—'

'She's mad!' Laura screamed. 'Completely barking.'

'Maybe, but she's harping back to that letter Paul sent Melissa—'

'That was ages ago! Just after she dumped him!'

Laura knew about the letter. The Kingsley-Porters had handed it over to the police, the day after Paul and

Melissa disappeared. Along with other bits of 'evidence' about their relationship.

The letter was harmless. Full of the usual teenage angst. And OK, so there'd been a few recriminations about how Paul felt let down. But nothing spiteful. Hardly hate mail! Especially under the circumstances.

Melissa wasn't like other girls. She didn't simply get fed up and end a relationship. Oh no. She had to create a whole flaming pantomime, didn't she? Casting Paul as the poor, deluded simpleton who saw aliens and herself as the mistreated heroine! And people actually fell for it. Sympathising with Melissa when it was Paul who got dumped, teased and taunted.

'Then there was that fight Paul got into,' her mother added. 'Melissa's parents say—'

'I don't care what they say! I don't care what Melissa told them, at the time! That wasn't Paul's fault!' said Laura. 'He didn't start it! He was the one who ended up with a black eye and a bruised rib while their saintly daughter stood there laughing, remember?'

'I don't think saintly's what you called her at the time,' said her mother, smiling faintly.

'No. I called her a scheming, venomous little bitch, if I remember rightly. And what did Paul do? Defended her, as usual. It wasn't Melissa's fault. She'd got in with the wrong crowd! Paul would have defended Melissa if he'd caught her, red-handed, skinning cats and roasting babies on spits! So don't you or Melissa's parents or anyone try to tell me he hated her. He didn't. Not ever. Not even for a single minute.'

Chapter 7

PAUL

Wrong again, Laura. But you wouldn't believe me, even if I could tell you, would you? Because girls always have to be right, don't they?

But you don't know everything, Laura. You don't know how much I can hear, do you? You don't know that every word you speak is forcing me to remember things I'd rather forget. You don't know how much you're hurting me.

Oh, it's OK. I'm not getting at you! I love you really. In my own, funny little way. Not that I'm going to tell you that. Even when I can speak again. My brain's not quite that warped, thank you very much.

Besides, I don't need to tell you, do I? You know we're close. Always have been. That's part of the problem, isn't it?

Oh sure we argue. All the time, in fact. You don't like me playing my drums when you're trying to watch 'EastEnders' and I can't bear you singing 'It's Raining Men' at the top of your painfully tuneless voice.

You get hysterical when I use the last of your shampoo, and I'm not keen on you borrowing my razor to do an emergency trim on your armpits. I mean, can you blame me? Yukky or what? But that's not your worst habit. Your worst habit is sticking your beak in my business, especially where Melissa's concerned. And you say mine's borrowing money and never paying it back.

Your pet names for me are 'motor mouth' and 'brainless prat' but let anyone else have a go at me and you're there, spitting and snarling like a mentally unbalanced leopard. Well, OK, maybe not so much now. But when I was little and used to get teased a lot about my eczema.

Oh, I remember you, out in the park or the playground, lecturing other kids about how it was cruel to tease people just because they were a bit different. And, if they wouldn't listen to reason, then you'd just give them a sneaky kick on the shin or pull their hair, wouldn't you?

And don't think I wasn't grateful. I was, at the time. When my own confidence and self-esteem were so pathetically low, I couldn't stick up for myself. But you've never quite realised things have changed, have you? I've grown up now. I can take care of myself. Even before my vision cleared and my eczema went away I was getting better, more confident, more able to fight my own battles. But you never quite got that, did you? You were still as protective towards me as you are to Jenna.

Trouble is, me having eczema made you a bit OVER-protective, I reckon. It sort of colours your view of me. You spent too many years thinking of me as a victim. So you could never imagine me as the villain of the piece,

58

could you? And if you caught ME skinning cats and roasting babies on spits, as you put it, you'd make some excuse for me, wouldn't you?

Well that's good, Laura. Because I think you're going to have to. If they go ahead with this hypnosis thing, they're talking about. If I start blurting things out...

Oh shit! Scary idea, this hypnosis. Really scary. Don't let them do it, Laura. I'm not ready. I'm not well enough. I haven't even worked it out myself yet. I know something happened. Something terrible. But I don't know what. I'm still locked in the past. Around the time that Melissa dumped me. Trying to remember how it felt.

Not too bad, I reckon. Considering. I mean it wasn't like I was deeply in love or anything. Lust maybe, but not love. So after a week or two of moping, I pulled myself round. Yeah, I'm sure, it wasn't any longer than that, though you probably wouldn't agree, Laura. You'd want to make out like Melissa broke my heart or something, wouldn't you?

She didn't. And losing Melissa wasn't the worst thing. The worst thing was the teasing. People having a laugh about my aliens. But by the end of term, even that was all forgotten. Because other bits of scandal had surfaced by then, giving people something else to gossip about.

Like that Year 9 girl getting pregnant. And nobody noticing till she collapsed in assembly and gave birth two days later. Then there were the A-level candidates who were accused of cheating in the maths exam and had their papers cancelled. And the major, major fuss over those lads selling cannabis plants at the school fête! You actually bought one for Mum, didn't you, Laura? For her herb garden! Naive or what?

I thought it was well funny but the Head was going ballistic! Three negative school stories appearing in the local paper in as many months! The emergency birth even made the Sunday tabloids. So alien abductions were definitely ancient history by the start of the summer holidays.

Melissa and I were ancient history too, no matter what you thought, Laura. We'd speak in class and, of course, I still fancied her. Who didn't? But she'd had two boyfriends since me. One in the Upper Sixth and one who she'd met at a show-jumping event.

I don't think anyone ever saw the horsey one but Melissa talked about him a lot. Or, at least, about how rich his family were. How they had a country house, complete with swimming pool, flat in London, holiday home in Portugal and a small yacht.

Melissa was supposed to be spending the first two weeks of the summer holidays with Mr-Super-Rich at the London flat. I don't know what happened. Who dumped who. But, at the start of the hols Melissa was still around. And that's when she got in with those bikers who'd pitched their tents on one of the local campsites.

You had a lot to say about that, at the time, Laura. Everybody did. How Melissa was asking for trouble hanging about with guys who were at least ten years older than her. Riding around on the back of their bikes, without a crash helmet. Different bike, different bloke, every day. Getting up to goodness knows what in their tents, at night.

But it wasn't as bad as everyone thought. I saw it, up close, remember? 'Cos I'd got a summer job at the campsite, hadn't I? Thanks to you doing your big sister act again. You were going out with Boring Barry Braithewaite from 'Young Farmers', at the time, who'd happened to mention that his dad needed a bit of cheap labour on his campsite.

So there I was, every day, cleaning the loos and trudging round with a black bin liner, picking up litter trying to make sure Melissa didn't see me. I mean I didn't look exactly cool with my mop and bottle of Cif, did I?

Especially compared to Melissa in her tight black trousers, red leather jacket and...yes...a crash helmet.

OK, so Melissa's parents weren't keen on what she was doing, but they bought her all the gear soon enough. Once they realised she'd go on the bikes with or without their blessing. And who could blame her? Some of the bikes were pretty neat. Which is what got me into trouble, of course.

You know, as well as anybody, what I'm like about machines, Laura. Sure I'd managed to keep a low profile when people were around but I just couldn't resist it that morning when I came across that bike parked outside the loos. The bikers had already gone off for the day and I wondered why one of them had left his bike behind. It wasn't unusual for the bikers to double up if there was a problem with one of their bikes but there certainly didn't seem to be anything wrong with the bike outside the loo. Far from it!

It was a Yamaha. Metallic blue with purple wheel trim and twin exhausts. Talk about dream machine. It had that carbon fibre bodywork that looks like honeycomb. The sort you can't resist running your hands along. Wow!

Can you imagine what it's like to ride one of those things, Laura? I could. Which is why I had to sit on it. Clutching the handlebars, swaying from side to side, making engine noises, like I was four years old or something!

'Vrooom, vrraaa, vrraaa . . .'

And that's when this great ape in leathers came out of the loo. He'd already hauled me off the bike and had me pinned up against the wall, when Melissa came out of the Ladies and burst out laughing.

That's when she laughed, Laura. Not later, like you make out when you're telling this story. You weren't there. You didn't see it.

'Oh, put him down, Neil,' Melissa drawled. 'Let's get going.'

But Ape-man wasn't listening. He was yelling, spitting in my face and, if I filter out all the obscenities, the general gist of the message was that I'd touched his bike. And he didn't like people touching his bike.

'Yeah, well I'm sure Paul's sorry,' said Melissa, still giggling. 'Aren't you, Paul?'

And maybe I should have apologised, like Melissa said, but the guy was huge! I was scared. Tried to wriggle past, push him away.

Before I knew it, I was on the ground, with a heavy boot smashing into my stomach, chest and face.

It might have been worse, only Mr Braithewaite came rushing out of his office in response to my screams. And when Melissa told him I'd started it, I guess, technically, she was being honest. I'd mucked with Ape-man's property, hadn't I? I'd pushed his shoulders. Maybe even caught his ankle with my foot. Not that he'd have felt anything through those boots.

I did though! The attack only lasted a couple of seconds but it felt like I'd been dropped from a cliff onto a bed of nails before being trampled by a herd of stampeding mammoths.

Boy, were you mad when you saw me that night, Laura. Mad with Mum for not taking me straight up to the hospital. Mad with Barry's dad for telling me it was best if I didn't work there anymore. Mad with me for refusing to tell the police. And, well, you know what you said about Melissa, don't you? Honestly, your language was worse than Ape-man's.

And that's why I ended up defending her. Because you were being so horrible and bitchy about her, as usual. But it wasn't the truth, Laura. It wasn't the way I felt. I couldn't believe what Melissa had told Barry's dad. I couldn't believe that she'd driven off on the back of that bike, while I was still lying there, gushing blood from my nose, puking onto the grass.

I thought she'd at least phone. Call round. See how I was. But she didn't. And I lay in bed that night, cold compress on my eyes, hot-water bottle on my ribs, cursing her, wishing her dead. Her and the Ape-man.

You don't know that though, Laura. 'Cos I only ever told one other person and it wasn't you. And even if you did know, you'd swear I didn't really mean it, wouldn't you? That I was just worked up, upset. But it was more than that.

I remember lying there, my good eye open, watching it unfold. Like I was directing a film. Following the twists and turns of a winding lane, seeing the metallic blue Yamaha miss a corner, skid up the bank, turn over into a ditch. Wheels spinning next to two bleeding, lifeless bodies.

And all the time I was grinning. Smiling at my own, private, little snuff movie. Letting my eyes settle on Melissa lying there, perfectly still.

Have you ever done that, Laura? Have you ever wished anyone dead? Do you know what it feels like? No? Well I'll tell you. It felt good, Laura! Good to be getting my own back. And it didn't even feel like fantasy. It felt too dark, too real. Like I was really wanting it to happen. Making it happen. Pretty sick, eh? Especially...

Oh God! It's all coming back now. And I don't want it to. I don't want to remember what happened just four days later.

It wasn't my fault. It wasn't! I didn't predict it. I didn't mean it. I didn't do it. I couldn't have done. It was an accident.

Ape-man wasn't involved at all. Nor was the Yamaha. It

was another bike. Another guy. The one they called Pandy. It didn't have anything to do with a ditch or a winding lane. It happened on a straight stretch. On a fine day. There was plenty of room. No reason for the bike to swerve, even with that van overtaking on the other side of the road. But it did. Hit the crash barrier. Burst into flames. Pandy died in hospital five hours later and Melissa . . .

You saw it on the local news, Laura. And I remember the way you looked when you came to tell me. How I felt. And we didn't even know then how bad it was going to be.

Melissa was in intensive care. And you tried to tell me, Laura, that she'd be OK. And I tried to believe you.

Only it got more difficult as the weeks went by. When Melissa was moved from intensive care to a private hospital. When she wouldn't see anyone. Not even her own parents, at first.

Nobody seemed to know anything. Not for ages. I couldn't phone her parents. I just couldn't. Besides, it wouldn't have done any good. They wouldn't speak to any of Melissa's friends. We tried phoning the hospital. Took it in turns to phone each week but all we ever got out of them was 'Melissa's comfortable' or 'Melissa's making progress'.

Progress! Oh sure. It all started to come out when we went back to school in September and the Head of Year 11 got us all together.

Melissa was still in hospital. Would probably be there for another month, at least. And, even once she was home, it was unlikely that she'd be coming back to school before Christmas. Meanwhile, it would be nice if we could organise a collection. Send her some flowers.

What did he think we'd all been doing? The florist barely had anything left and the stationer's was clean out of Get Well cards. But we made the collection. Sent an enormous bouquet. Wrote e-mails, sent letters and cards by the bagful but we never got any replies.

Rumours spread like some manic game of Chinese Whispers.

'Mrs Fairley, from the surgery, says the doctor's round there nearly every day.'

'My mum saw Melissa's parents dumping some stuff at the tip. It was mirrors. All mirrors. They must have taken every mirror out of the house!'

'Melissa's been to see a plastic surgeon. Down in London.'

'That's not what I heard. I heard she was being treated for depression.'

'No. She's having another operation on her spine.'

Every rumour twisted round my gut like a knife. I don't want to make this about me. I don't want to dredge up all the guilt again. But that's how I felt. Guilty about my disgusting daydream. Guilty about wishing Melissa dead. Almost believing that my thoughts had, somehow, reached out, made it happen. And I guess I wasn't easy to live with. My concentration was shot to pieces. I couldn't sleep. I was causing row after row at home. You got the worst of it, Laura. And you just took it all. For ages. Until that day I had a major go at Jenna.

It was November 5th. Bonfire night. You'd promised to take Jenna to the bonfire down at the community centre. But Jenna was too excited to wait. Kept pestering me to light sparklers for her. I'd told her a dozen times to buzz off. I was busy. But she kept coming back, whining at me in that high-pitched squeak she has, dumping her sparklers on top of my homework till in the end I lost it. Lost it completely. Picked up the sparklers and snapped the whole lot in half. Then, when she started crying, I grabbed her shoulders and shook her.

That's when you came in. Pulled Jenna away from me and belted me across the face.

'Don't ever, ever, touch Jenna again,' you yelled, as poor Jenna stood there shaking, screaming for Mum. 'I know what this is about, Paul, but it's gone on long enough. I'm not going to stand by and watch that bloody girl ruin our lives. She's ruined her own life. Isn't that enough, Paul? Isn't it?'

That was the only time I remember you ever getting really mad at me, Laura. And even then, you somehow managed to blame Melissa, didn't you?

But it made me think. And I knew I had to do something. Before I flipped completely. I had to see her. I had to find out for myself.

So the following day, I went round there, straight after school. I didn't tell anyone I was going. Didn't phone the Kingsley-Porters to check whether it was OK because I knew it wouldn't be.

I just marched up to the door and rang the bell.

Melissa's mother answered the door but I didn't recognise her at first. She looked sort of small, hunched, weary. And I don't think she recognised me for a minute, either. Then it clicked.

'What do you want?'

'I've come to see Melissa.'

'Why?'

That threw me for a second. The word and the look.

'We're friends . . . I want to see—'

'Well, you can't! What do you think it is? Some sort of peepshow? For people to gawp at. So you can rush back to school and tell everyone how she . . . how she—'

I didn't know what to do when Melissa's mum started to cry. It wasn't just ordinary tears. Her whole body started to shake and I honestly thought she was going to collapse. She probably would have done, if I hadn't grabbed hold of her arm. I could feel the full force of her weight slumped against me, as I steered her inside.

I'd remembered there was a chair just inside the hall by the full-length mirror with the fancy frame. The mirror had gone but fortunately the chair was still there.

'You'd better go now,' she said, clutching the arms of the chair. 'Please. It's best.'

'Who is it?'

Melissa's voice. Or rather a duller, flatter version of the voice I knew. Coming from the lounge.

'It's Paul,' I said. 'Paul Crompton.'

'Wait a minute,' she shouted. 'Don't move. Don't come in.'

Something of the old drama in the voice that time. Something reassuringly like the old Melissa.

'Please go,' her mother said again.

But it was too late. Melissa was already coming out of the lounge, propelling herself towards me in her wheel-chair.

And the worst thing is, I know these memories aren't the end of the story. They're only the beginning. What I'm blocking out, what I'm still refusing to see is...is...no...It's too soon. I'm not ready. Don't look at me like that, Melissa. Leave me alone! It wasn't my fault. Go away! Leave me alone!

No. Don't go. I didn't mean it!

'Melissa!'

Chapter 8

Laura paced up and down in the reception area, late on Friday afternoon, waiting for Paul to return. So much had happened in the last hour. After living their lives in slow motion for the past five days, everything had suddenly speeded up, like a video on fast forward. And Laura was desperately trying to re-play it, in her head, trying to slow it down.

She and her mum had been sitting with Paul, waiting for Dad to turn up, waiting for the hypno-therapist. Talking quietly, at first, so as not to disturb Paul, then not talking at all. Just sitting. Picking up magazines. Putting them down again. It was almost totally silent in the little room, so they both heard it. Heard it quite clearly. The first real word Paul had spoken.

'Melissa.'

They'd both raced over to his chair. Laura had knelt on the floor and he'd said it again.

'Melissa.'

'Paul?' Laura had urged. 'Can you hear me? Do you know where she is? Can you tell us about Melissa?'

'It didn't happen.'

Torn between distress and elation, Laura had rushed

70

out. Told the duty nurse, who had, in turn, informed the doctor.

Everyone had agreed, it was a good sign. But any hopes Laura might have had, that it would mean delaying the hypnosis, were quickly squashed. To the doctor's mind, it meant that the hypnosis had more chance of success.

Well, he was the professional. He should know. And Laura had no choice but to trust his judgement. All kinds of safety procedures had been put in place. The sessions would be short. They would be taped. The first session would deal only in generalities, while the therapist tried to establish trust and assess whether Paul was receptive. At the first sign of any problem, Paul would be brought round.

'People have misconceived ideas about hypnotic regression,' the doctor had said. 'It isn't about delving or prying. It's not something which is "done" to a patient. It will be a co-operative venture between Dr Kapra and Paul. She won't force anything on him. The patient is always in control.'

Laura wished she felt in control. But she didn't. Not of anything anymore. She looked at her parents, standing talking by the window. They were probably discussing all the things which were spinning round in her own head. Paul. Melissa's parents. Melissa.

Trust that to be the name Paul had called out. Not Mum or Dad or Jenna or Laura. But Melissa.

Could the Kingsley-Porters be right? Had Paul developed some sort of unhealthy obsession with their daughter? If he had, it had only happened since the accident. Sure, he'd liked her before. Maybe more than liked her. But Laura doubted whether it was real love. And it certainly wasn't obsession.

But after the accident. Well, that was different. For a start, Paul was the only person Melissa would see. Apart from her parents and medical staff. And, though Melissa's parents hadn't been too keen at first, they soon began to encourage Paul to go round at every opportunity.

Paul gave them a break from Melissa and, by the time of his first visit, in November, they certainly needed it. It couldn't have been easy to cope with a daughter who was paralysed. Especially one as demanding as Melissa.

There are some people, Laura reflected, who cope with disabilities. Battling on, ignoring them, or treating them as a challenge. But not Melissa.

It would have been hard enough for a girl like Melissa to come to terms with being in a wheelchair. But she might have learnt to cope, in time, Laura thought. If it hadn't been for the other stuff. The burns. The scars on her body. On her face.

Melissa wouldn't let anyone see her face. Couldn't bear to look at it herself. Until Paul managed to talk her round, she wouldn't even leave the house unless it was to go to the hospital or the London clinic. And then she insisted on having curtains drawn in the back of the car. And she always, always, wore a hat with a veil.

Still the same old dramatic Melissa, Laura had thought when Paul had told her about the hat. Hiding away like a mysterious heroine from a gothic novel. Only this was no melodrama. This was for real and Laura had felt, with a sudden sickness, that she had no right to criticise. Maybe she'd be the same in similar circumstances. Maybe she'd be worse. How could you possibly know?

Who could blame Melissa for alternately screaming and shouting, then lapsing into the bleak, silent depressions which drove her parents to breaking point.

Yet Paul seemed able to cope with Melissa's violent mood swings. He was unbelievable. Going round there almost every day. Sometimes all day at weekends. Sometimes staying overnight, if Melissa was particularly bad. If her parents couldn't handle it.

Paul couldn't always talk Melissa round. Often, he'd just sit there, letting her scream, holding her if she was about to do herself harm. But if there were any breakthroughs to be made, it was Paul who made them.

One night, in the middle of November, when it was overcast and very dark, Melissa let him wheel her outside into the garden for the first real breath of fresh air she'd had in four months. The following night, he took her right to the end of the street. By early December Melissa was venturing to the outskirts of town or down onto the coast if the tide was out and the sea wasn't too rough. But only at night. Nothing anyone could do or say would persuade Melissa to go out during daylight.

Mum and Dad had been worried about Paul. Often he wasn't coming home until the early hours of the morning. They were worried that his school work would suffer in the vital GCSE year. But Paul would only snap and say that all his work was up to date. That it was his life. He could do what he wanted with it. And Mum and Dad had shrugged, given up. After all there were worse things a sixteen-year-old could choose to do.

But was it normal? Was it normal for a sixteen-year-old to devote so much time to a friend who'd been injured in an horrific accident? Or was it, as Melissa's parents had since tried to claim, something obsessive, sinister?

Laura didn't have time to analyse further. Life was moving on again. A nurse was bringing Paul back. Paul paused, smiled at Laura. A relaxed, easy smile. Surely a good sign?

The first session, the therapist assured them later, as they prepared to listen to the tape, had gone well. Far better than expected. Paul had been quite tense but receptive. And, most importantly, he had quite effortlessly broken through the barrier and spoken.

Laura thought she could understand why. The therapist, Dr Kapra, was a plump, pleasant-faced woman, with remarkably soft green eyes and a voice which could surely calm a storm.

Even when Dr Kapra was speaking normally, her voice had a soothing, soporific quality, so goodness knows what it was like when she was into the hypnosis.

'What I need you to do,' she purred, 'is listen to the tape and see if you can verify any of the incidents Paul talks about. 'We need to establish which are true memories and which might be false.'

'False?' said Mrs Crompton. 'You mean Paul might have lied?'

'Oh no. But we have to be very careful. Not all memories are true. Some might be dream or fantasy related. Something the patient has seen on a film or read in a book can become mixed with reality. Or they might talk out one of their own fantasies, seeing it as reality.'

'So, if some of the things they say aren't true,' said Laura, 'what's the point?'

'The point is to help the patient,' said Dr Kapra. 'I want to help Paul work through the things which are clearly troubling him. And, if anything he says can help the police find the girl, all well and good. But my main aim is to help Paul.'

Help Paul. The words, especially purred in that way, were reassuring.

'Now, you may find some of the things he says are a bit strange,' said the therapist, immediately destroying Laura's sense of wellbeing. 'But I hope you can help me to establish where they might be coming from.'

Laura had to try hard to focus, as the tape began. Stop herself going under, along with Paul, as the therapist's voice talked of warmth, security, relaxation.

'I think you feel happy now, don't you, Paul?' came the voice. 'Can you tell me where you are?'

'I'm in the garden, with Poppy.'

Poppy, Laura thought. The neighbour's cat, when they'd lived in Sheffield. Before Jenna was born. Before they'd moved here. So Paul could only have been what?

Three, four years old? A true memory, from way back. She didn't say so though. They'd been asked to listen to the whole tape first. Then they could go back to the beginning. Tackle it in sections.

There were a lot of true memories in there, they were able to tell Dr Kapra at the end. The cat. The park. The day Mum brought Jenna home. Funny how Paul remembered all the details of that, Laura thought. He hadn't seemed to take much notice at the time.

There were a couple of minor references they couldn't place. Who was the 'Luke' he talked about? Paul had never had a friend called Luke. Unless perhaps it was Luke Skywalker out of *Star Wars*. Paul had been through a phase of believing he WAS Luke Skywalker when he was little. Waving his light sabre around. Saving the world!

And where was 'the stream with the stepping stones'? That one had thrown them completely. They had no idea.

Dr Kapra was puzzled when Paul began to moan about the itching. Kids taunting him in class for 'scratching his fleas'.

'Paul had chronic eczema,' Dad explained.

'But he doesn't have it now?' asked Dr Kapra.

'No, he doesn't have it now.'

Then, near the end of the tape, the bit they all found strange. Dr Kapra had been trying to draw him out a bit about the itching. Trying to get him to talk about how it felt when he was being teased. And the shy, self-conscious Paul, whom Laura remembered, was back. Talking about staring out of the classroom window, watching the other children play. Scared to go out. Knowing he couldn't join in their games. It was worse than even Laura had imagined. The sense of isolation. Of being different. But then suddenly, mid-memory, Paul's voice had changed, becoming angry, bitter.

'But it was nothing! I wasn't crippled. I wasn't disabled. It was sores, that's all. Not burns. Not scars. Not like . . .'

Dr Kapra was going to bring him round, at that point. When he'd jumped to the present. When he was clearly thinking about Melissa. But then his voice had changed again, becoming so light, so carefree, it was almost a song.

'They made it better. They didn't want to hurt me. I didn't have to be frightened. I wouldn't feel anything. Watch the ripples. All I had to do was watch the ripples. I can still see them. All the lovely colours. Changing. Melissa's seen them too. She's seen the colours.'

All Laura and her parents could do was shake their heads. It didn't mean anything to them. Paul had once had a lamp. One of those lava lamp things with undulating colours. Maybe he was remembering that. But it didn't explain where Melissa fitted in. Or who 'they' were.

'Maybe I'll try to explore that tomorrow,' Dr Kapra said. 'See if we can take him back to the colours.'

Chapter 9

PAUL

The nurse has just ask me if I want a drink. I tried to answer but it wouldn't come out, so I didn't force it. A nod got me my drink but I can't go on nodding or shaking forever. I've got to try to speak. Of my own accord.

The thing is, I'm still bothered about this hypnosis. Oh, it's not as scary or weird as you might think. I always thought hypnotists took over your brain. Made you do daft things. Jump around like a frog, eat tulips or sing the National Anthem backwards. And I thought that when you came round, you didn't remember any of it. Didn't know why people were falling about laughing.

Maybe that's a different sort of hypnotism. Different from what Dr Kapra does, anyway. She didn't swing a watch in front of my eyes or tell me I was getting sleepy or any of the stuff you see on TV. She just talked and, after a while, when I could feel the iceberg melting, I talked too.

Only, it didn't feel like me. It felt like someone else. Somewhere else. And that's the problem, isn't it? The someone else took over. I knew what he was saying but I couldn't stop him. Because I was too tired, by then. Too relaxed. Too sleepy. So I just sat there, letting him chatter on. I even let him mention Melissa.

So I'm not really in control, am I? Dr Kapra said I would be. And I think she believes that. But I didn't feel in control. Not once we'd got going. And I'd still rather tell it my own way. If I could. Even though part of me knows that they'd send me to prison. Or a psychiatric unit. If they knew what I'd done. But how could they when I'm not even sure myself?

Maybe if I could just make them understand what it was like for Melissa, after the accident...

Oh, everybody thought I was marvellous, going round there day after day. Taking Melissa on midnight excursions in her wheelchair. Sitting with her even when she raged, screamed, threw things, cried.

Saint Paul. Has a nice sort of ring to it, don't you think?

Only I wasn't a saint. Far from it. Because it wasn't really about helping Melissa. It was about helping me. And I didn't always get things right. In fact, I got it hopelessly wrong, at first. Like Melissa's parents.

They were sure that Melissa would learn to cope in time. With the help of a physiotherapist, counsellor, plastic surgeon. The army of medical people they paid for.

They tried to point out all the things Melissa could still do. Her brain wasn't impaired. She could go back to school, or study at home with a tutor if she wanted to. Still get her qualifications.

'What's the point?' she'd say, wearily. 'What's the point of GCSEs and A-levels, when you can't even walk? What am I supposed to do when I've got them?'

'Being in a wheelchair doesn't stop you going to

college, university,' her dad would say.

'It stops me going to drama school, doesn't it, though?' she'd scream at them. 'I wanted to go to drama school but they're not going to take me now, are they? Equal rights don't stretch that far, do they? Taking on a girl who can only play an invalid or bit parts in horror films. I suppose I could point out what they'd save on make-up.'

Sounds sort of funny. The kind of joke people used to make when my eczema was bad. But, of course, with Melissa, it was no joke. Her life, as far as she was concerned, was over.

Which is why it wasn't only the mirrors that were cleared out. Melissa's parents had to move all the knives out of reach. All the pills that Melissa's mum took for her headaches. All Melissa's own medication. Because, given half a chance, Melissa would have swallowed the lot.

The thing that got Melissa really mad, was if anyone tried to point out that there were loads of people worse off than her. Once, Melissa's dad tried to show her a newspaper article about a young boy. A haemophiliac who'd been infected with HIV, through a blood transfusion. He was so brave, that lad. Campaigning to make transfusions safer. Going on TV, trying to break down some of the prejudice against AIDS sufferers.

'What a hero,' Melissa had screamed. 'What a pity I'm not like him. Or like all the other bloody heroes you've told me about. The ones who play basketball from their wheelchairs or clump up mountains with their walking frames. Oh, you'd like that, wouldn't you? Then you could show me off again, couldn't you? She might be grotesque but see how brave she is?'

'Melissa, you're not grotesque,' her dad tried to say. 'Especially not since the last lot of surgery—'

'Oh sure! I look great now I've had half my backside grafted onto my face. Lovely if you happen to want a face that looks like your bum. Would you like to see their handiwork, Paul? Would you like to see what they've done?'

Before I could answer, or even think, Melissa was lifting the veil. Showing me her face, for the very first time since the accident.

Not much time to prepare but I tried. Knowing I mustn't show the slightest hint of shock, revulsion. Remembering how I used to feel if someone shuddered as they accidentally brushed my hand or if they turned their eyes from my face.

It was easier than I thought. Melissa's dad was right. It wasn't grotesque. Not even close up. Her eyes were still huge and strikingly blue, though her brows and lashes still hadn't grown back properly. Her hair was shorter than before, framing the sides of her face, to hide some of the scarring, I guessed. Some of the skin looked discoloured, patchy, tightly dawn but you could tell it was healing. There'd been more bone damage on the left than the right so she'd need more surgery to restore symmetry.

Breaking it down like that, it sounds bad. And it was. I don't want to give the impression that Melissa was making a big fuss over nothing. But, the thing is, another person would have reacted differently. Been pleased that the surgeons had been able to do so much in a relatively short time. Showed more confidence in them. More optimism.

The medical team had even produced computer generated graphics of what she'd look like after twelve months of treatment, eighteen months, two years. They hadn't tried to cheat or pretend she'd be absolutely back to what she'd been. But, honestly, those pictures would have been good enough to have most people, in Melissa's position, waving their arms and cheering.

But Melissa wasn't most people. And it was no good trying to pretend she was. All the lecturing, all the cajoling, all the reasoning were a waste of time. She couldn't suddenly change her personality. None of us can do that. Sounds obvious, doesn't it? But it sure took me a long time to realise. Weeks of blundering. Making things worse.

'So what do you think, Paul?' she'd said. 'Still fancy me? Think anyone could ever fancy me?'

How could I answer that? Anything I'd said would have been wrong. 'No' for obvious reasons. 'Yes', because Melissa wouldn't have believed me. So I made my biggest mistake of all. It was so pathetic, I feel embarrassed just thinking about it.

'Fancying people isn't just about how they look, is it?' I said, remembering all the stuff my parents and Laura used to say to me. 'I mean, you look OK and you'll look great again, once they've finished all the surgery but even if you didn't, people would still love you. For what you are. For what's inside.'

'Don't!' Melissa had screamed. 'Don't give me that crap, Paul. You, of all people. You know bloody well it isn't true. Do you think people would have fancied you if you'd still had great flakes of dry skin peeling from your face and those ugly red blotches all over the place? Do you think Ellie would have gone out with you . . . or that I would!'

'Maybe not so soon,' I said, as honestly as I could. 'And you, maybe, not ever. But Ellie, yes. Other girls, yes. Once we'd all grown up a bit. I think there are loads of people who are capable of seeing beyond the physical. The odd blotch or blemish or even major handicap. There are loads of people with disabilities out there. They've got husbands, wives, lovers, children—'

'Oh, have they?' Melissa snarled. 'Well, maybe, it's like you say, Paul. Maybe they've got something else. Wit, intelligence, determination, some sort of inner beauty. Maybe they're nice inside. But what if you're me? What if you're not even nice inside? What if the inside is even worse than the mangled bloody mess on the outside? What then, Paul?'

'That's not true,' I said. 'You are nice.'

Nice. I actually used that word. The one you're not supposed to use in school essays. Even as I said it, I could imagine our English teacher, Mrs Laine, hovering behind me.

'Can't you think of a better word than that, Paul? Nice doesn't mean much, does it? What is it you really want to say?'

83

And, above the whisper of Mrs Laine's imaginary voice came the scream of Melissa's real one.

'Well it shows how deep you looked, doesn't it, Paul? You've known me all your life and what have you ever seen, eh? Beyond the blonde hair and big boobs? Nothing! You haven't seen anything, have you? Because if you had, you'd know! You'd know I can't live like this. With people gawping at me, pitying me, patronising me. I'd rather be dead. Have you got that? I'd rather be dead!'

She meant it too. Hearing her scream it over and over was bad enough but the pleading was worse. On Christmas Day, I got a phone call from Melissa's parents. I'd promised to go round there in the evening but this was two o'clock. Just as Mum was about to serve lunch. I was starving but I went anyway. Grabbing a drumstick and a couple of roast potatoes on my way out.

Bit different in Melissa's house to ours. There wasn't a centimetre of wall or ceiling in our house that hadn't been covered in streamers, cards, balloons or garish glittery collages that Jenna had made at school. In Melissa's house, nothing. Not even a tree.

No wonder Melissa was depressed.

'I wanted to put the cards up, at least,' her mother said, apologetically. 'But she wouldn't let me. She won't do anything, eat anything, say anything. She won't even get out of bed. She's just lying there, crying.'

She wasn't crying when I went into the downstairs room, which was now Melissa's bedroom. In fact she smiled at me when I went in, and it did cross my mind that it had all been an act, a ploy, to get me there. She wasn't wearing her veil and kept running her hands across her face, tracing the uneven surfaces with her fingers.

'Get me a drink,' she said.

'What do you want?'

'Gin and tonic. Ice. Slice of lemon. Not too much tonic.'

'Er, your parents won't let me bring you alcohol,' I said, wondering whether she was joking. 'Not on an empty stomach and with all the pills you're taking.'

'Yes they will! It's Christmas. I want to celebrate. Tell them I want to celebrate!'

Her dad poured the drink. Tiniest splash of gin. Two ice cubes. Half a bottle of tonic. And the lemon.

'Aren't you having anything?' she asked, as I delivered it.

'No. I'm OK.'

She sipped her drink, just looking at me, for a while.

'I've been thinking,' she said, eventually. 'It wouldn't be that difficult, you know. Don't tell them, but I've been storing up some of my tablets already. All I'd need was a couple of packets of headache pills or something. Bottle of gin or whisky. You could get those for me, couldn't you, Paul?'

'No!' I said, instinctively, before I'd even wrapped my brain round what she was saying.

'They'd never know,' she said. 'You wouldn't get into trouble. I could leave a note. Say how I'd somehow managed to get hold of the stuff myself . . .'

'Melissa, you don't mean any of this. Not really.'

85

I expected her to start yelling at me but she didn't. She just smiled, placidly.

'Remember that rabbit we found out on the school field when we were in top juniors?' she said.

I nodded. It wasn't the sort of thing you'd forget. Poor thing had been mauled... by a dog, probably. Half its guts were hanging out but it was still alive.

'We screamed for the caretaker and we wanted him to take it to the vet, didn't we?'

I nodded again.

'But he said it was past help. It was a wild animal. It would be wrong to let it suffer anymore. And he sent us all back into school, telling us he'd deal with it. He'd make sure he did it quickly. It wouldn't feel any pain.'

'And the whole lot of us spent the afternoon in tears,' I said. 'While Miss Halliday tried to tell us it was for the best.'

'And she was right, wasn't she?'

'We're talking about a rabbit, Melissa. An animal.'

'So we should be kinder to animals than we are to people, is that what you're saying? We shouldn't let them suffer but it's all right for people?'

'No,' I hissed, aware of footsteps outside the room. 'It was different. That rabbit was dying anyway. Mr Cox only speeded it up.'

'Can I get you anything?' Melissa's mother asked, hovering by the door. 'Mince pie? Piece of cake?'

'No. No thank you,' I said, trying to stop myself retching.

As her mother left the room, Melissa smiled at me again.

'And what about that debate we did in Year 9, Paul? You and me on the same side. I mean, maybe not many people heard you, mumbling into your notes but I did. You put forward a cracking argument for euthanasia then, didn't you? People's freedom to choose. Basic human right.'

'You don't have to believe what you say in a debate! I only did it 'cos nobody else would volunteer. They were all against it.'

'At first,' Melissa pointed out. 'But the majority voted in favour, in the end, didn't they?'

'We were talking about very old people, Melissa. The terminally ill. And I still don't think half the class were convinced. They only voted in favour because of you!'

'Rubbish!'

'Melissa, you even got them to vote for cutting school holidays once! You could talk anybody into anything!'

That, of course, was the problem.

'I know,' Melissa said. 'That's how I know you'll do it for me. Maybe not now. Maybe not even next week, next month. But you will, Paul. You'll help me in the end.'

Was she right? Is that what I did? Is that what I'm blocking out? I don't think so. I wouldn't have done that. I couldn't have. There was another way. I know there was another way.

Chapter 10

Saturday afternoon. Laura stood helplessly watching a nurse feeding Paul another sedative as he rocked in her arms, muttering those words.

'It didn't happen.'

Why, oh why, hadn't she stopped them? Laura thought. She'd known, instinctively, that the hypnosis had been wrong. Why hadn't she made more of a stand?

That morning everything had looked so good. Mum had taken Jenna round to a friend's house while Laura and Dad had stayed chatting to Paul. Well, they'd chatted while Paul nodded and shook his head but it had been fine.

Paul had seemed quite happy, relaxed. The conversation had flowed. Some of Paul's nods and shakes had begun to have some expression to them. He was smiling more. Pulling faces. Raising his eyebrows. Using his hands in gestures. All progress. Communication.

So, after lunch, when Dr Kapra had come to take Paul off for his session, Laura hadn't been too worried. She and her parents had gone down to the café to get some lunch themselves.

They were still there, half an hour or so later, when the call came through for them. Could they go back up to the ward?

Dr Kapra had been calmly apologetic. The session hadn't gone too well. What an understatement that turned out to be!

Once they'd settled Paul, watched him fall asleep, they'd gone to listen to the tape.

'It might be difficult for you,' Dr Kapra had said. 'But try to listen to the whole tape, before we discuss it.'

Another understatement. It wasn't difficult. It was impossible.

Usual routine at the start. Dr Kapra talking quietly, establishing trust. Asking Paul's permission to relax him, take him deeper. Back to the colours perhaps? Could they talk about the lovely colours?

'I remembered,' said Paul. 'All the colours. I had to remember them. I had to bring them back. It was the only way.'

'You had to bring the colours back?' said Dr Kapra's voice.

'They came back,' said Paul. 'In the dreams. They'd never really gone away. And I was glad. I wanted them back. I didn't want to do what she said.'

Laura had found herself, leaning forward, close to the tape, not wanting to miss a word.

'I didn't want to get the tablets for her. I didn't want to. The rabbit was different. I told her, the rabbit was different!'

Agonising silence on the tape. Dr Kapra didn't ask or pry. So the next voice was Paul again.

'I didn't get them. I didn't. She kept asking me.

Shouting at me. Crying. I wasn't her friend. I wouldn't help her. Such a little thing, Paul. Why won't you do it for me? Just get me the bloody whisky then!'

'Melissa wanted you to get her tablets, whisky?' purred Dr Kapra's voice. 'Do you know why, Paul?'

'Isn't it obvious!' Laura had shouted out, unable to keep quiet. 'She was suicidal. She talked him into helping her! What has he done? What has he done?'

'Please,' said Dr Kapra, stopping the tape. 'Try to bear with it. Would you like a break, perhaps? Glass of water?'

Laura took the water. Sat back. Gripped the glass, tightly.

'She wanted to die,' were the first words Laura heard when the tape re-started. 'She wanted me to help her. She said it was all right.'

'What did you think, Paul?' Dr Kapra had asked, oh so quietly. 'Did you think it was all right?'

'I didn't know. I wasn't sure. There was something I had to do. I had to help her. It was all my fault. I had to.'

'What does he mean, his fault?' said Laura.

Her dad had got up, at that point, started to pace round the room.

Dr Kapra had stopped the tape again.

'Is that it?' said Laura's dad. 'Did you stop him? Did you bring him out?'

'He wasn't ready to come out,' said Dr Kapra. 'The patient makes the choices.'

Rubbish, Laura had wanted to say, but she didn't.

'He wanted to talk,' said Dr Kapra. 'Listen.'

90

She switched on the tape.

'How did you help her, Paul?' said the honey-trap voice. 'How did you help Melissa?'

'She didn't like my idea. She said I was crazy. The tablets, Paul. Just get me the tablets. I don't want you to show me, Paul. I don't want you to explain. Don't start all that again. There are no colours. No miracles. It didn't happen.'

'He's closing down,' said Laura's mother. 'He doesn't want to talk anymore.'

'No,' said Dr Kapra, patiently stopping the tape. 'I know it's confusing. But that's Melissa talking. Melissa's telling him something didn't happen.'

'So she planted that phrase in his mind?' said Laura. 'But why? What's she talking about? What didn't happen? What's going on?'

'I'm not sure,' said Dr Kapra. 'I was hoping you could tell me. The session's almost over. Just listen to the last bit. Tell me what you make of it.'

'I made her do it,' said Paul's voice, clearly agitated now. 'She didn't want to. She was scared. Of the sea and the waves. And the spiders. She hates spiders. They're not spiders, Melissa. You don't have to be scared. They're not spiders. Watch the colours. Hold on. I'm not crazy. I know what I'm doing. It's the only way. I know what I'm doing. I'm not crazy. They'll be there. Why aren't they here? It's cold. So cold. Why haven't they come? I can't see. I can't breathe. I can't move. I can't breathe. I can't see. Where is she? What have you done to her? It didn't happen! It didn't happen!'

Laura barely knew how she'd managed to listen as Paul's voice rose to an agonising scream. She'd rushed out of the room, gone back to Paul, leaving her parents with Dr Kapra, to try to talk, rationalise, analyse, explain.

How could you begin to make sense of it? How could you know what was truth and what was fiction? Who could say where the rabbits and spiders were coming from?

Other bits were easy, of course. Not hard to believe that Melissa had been suicidal. Asking for tablets and whisky. Not hard to imagine the strain it would have put Paul under. But why hadn't he mentioned it? Why had he tried to cope alone? Why hadn't he talked it through? Told Melissa's doctor? Her parents?

Maybe he had told Melissa's parents. Maybe they'd refused to believe it. Just like Laura's parents were refusing to believe some of the other stuff Paul had blurted out.

But the police might. If you combined Paul's ramblings with some of the other evidence, it might even start to make some sort of sense. Maybe.

Laura sat down on the end of Paul's bed. He was calmer again, after the second sedative of the day. Awake but not really focusing, so Laura fixed a placid sort of smile on her face as she tried to go over the sequence of events.

The wheelchair had been found first. On its side, under the rough wooden ramp which led down to the beach at the quieter, unfashionable, pebbly, muddy end. Then the clothes. The jacket and trainers. Only one jacket. Paul's. Melissa's had never been found.

That was the 'hard' evidence. There was more. A witness

had claimed to have seen a lad and a girl down there, one night. He wasn't sure whether it was Saturday. The kids were arguing, he said. Then the lad had lifted the screaming girl and walked right out into the sea. But the witness hadn't come forward till the Tuesday night. And the witness was Cider Joe, staggering into the police station in an unusually bad state, even for him. Raving about seeing a huge flying fish leaping in and out of the water, too. So his testimony was hardly what you'd call reliable.

No one else had seen Paul and Melissa but that wasn't unusual. That was the whole point of them going out late at night and keeping to isolated spots. So Melissa wouldn't be seen.

It hadn't, of course, struck Laura's parents as odd, that Paul wasn't back by midnight on Saturday, when they went to bed. Laura had been out with friends. A last, festive celebration before the college term started.

When she got home, around 3am, she had no idea whether Paul was back or not. She hadn't even thought about it. Her brain, awash with alcohol, hadn't been in a state to think about much . . . until the phone rang.

'Is Melissa there?'

'Er . . . sorry, no, I don't think so,' Laura had mumbled. 'Who's this?'

'Melissa's father. They're not back yet. Are they with you?'

Laura had sobered pretty quickly. Rushed upstairs, checked Paul's room, woken her parents.

They hadn't been too concerned, at first. Dad had got

the car out. Gone down to town. Tried the park. The coast road. Melissa's dad had done the same. Only when they found no sign of Paul and Melissa, did they call the police.

Teenage boys and girls going missing together might not always trigger a major and immediate police response but Melissa's condition and the insistence of her parents got a pretty fast reaction.

An overreaction, Laura had thought at first. She was sure that Paul and Melissa had simply tucked themselves away somewhere quiet to talk. Lost track of time. Fallen asleep, perhaps. She was managing to keep pretty calm, even in the face of rising hysteria from Melissa's parents, until they'd found the wheelchair, early on Sunday morning, as the tide went out.

It was almost impossible now, Laura thought, to remember everything clearly. What the police had found and when. Who they'd spoken to. Where they'd searched.

Somewhere along the line, they'd checked out all Paul and Melissa's friends and relatives. Organised a coastal search. Sent out boats and helicopters. Appealed for witnesses. Got Cider Joe.

Did Paul's ramblings suggest that Joe might have been right? Had they been down on the beach, arguing? Had Paul lifted Melissa, walked towards the sea ... Or ...

Laura paused, thinking about the other things Paul had said. What if Paul hadn't walked towards the sea? What if he'd walked in another direction? Back towards the rocks, the caves, the abandoned beach huts? Everything had been searched, of course, but they could have missed something. They'd missed Paul, hadn't they?

A cave, an old beach hut would be full of spiders. He'd definitely mentioned spiders. But why would he take Melissa somewhere like that? To do what she'd asked? To give her the tablets? To help her die?

Towards the sea. Away from the sea. Either way, it didn't look good. And none of it explained who 'they' were. Unless you believed Melissa's parents, which Laura didn't.

'It's all my fault,' Melissa's mother had screamed out during one of the early meetings with the police. 'I should have stopped him coming round. He's mad, you know. Delusional. Sees spaceships and little green men. And I let him loose with my daughter!'

'The alien thing was months ago,' Laura had tried to point out. 'And it was just a joke, anyway. A joke Melissa blew out of all proportion. Paul's not mad and you know it!'

'I'm not talking about months ago,' Mrs Kingsley-Porter had said. 'I'm talking about recently. Last week. Melissa told me that Paul had been on about his aliens again. He'd had her looking at Internet sites. Melissa thought it was hysterical. And I laughed with her. Happy to see her smiling again. I should have known. I should have known he was mad. Dangerous. Anyone who thinks he sees aliens is capable of anything.'

'Are you telling me that Paul thought he'd been in contact with aliens?' one of the policemen had said, looking understandably confused.

'Oh, it was worse than that,' Mrs Kingsley-Porter had screamed out. 'Do you want to know what he's been telling her? Do you want to know the rubbish he's been filling her head with?'

It had all come spilling out and Laura had sat there shaking her head. Wondering just who was mad. Who was making things up. Melissa? Melissa's mother? One thing she was sure of. It wasn't Paul. None of it had come from Paul. Paul was as sane as she was. And nothing he came out with under hypnosis was going to change her mind.

She looked at Paul, who seemed to have fallen asleep again, and then towards the door, knowing instinctively that someone was there. It was her parents, beckoning her.

'It's not looking good,' her father said.

'You can't go by someone's ramblings under hypnosis,' Laura pointed out. 'Even Dr Kapra said half of it could be pure fantasy.'

'It's not just that,' said her mother. 'Those tests that the police asked for on the scratches down Paul's arm—'

'Yes?' said Laura.

'They've had some results. The scratches were almost certainly made by Melissa.'

Chapter 11

PAUL

What have I done? What have I done? It was coming out all wrong. I knew it was. That's why I had to stop him. The other me who was talking.

Shit, I'm starting to sound crazy, even to myself.

Get a grip, Paul. Get a grip. It's all these pills they keep shovelling down your throat. Making you too tired to think.

They're talking about me out there. About the scratches. Well, I could explain that. Sort of. I think. Oh no. Laura's coming back in.

So breathe deeply. Sit up a bit. Smile at her. Make her think you're OK. That's better. Now think. What really happened? After Melissa started pestering you to get that stuff for her, what did you do?

I flipped. Panicked. That's what. Walked around for days, just thinking about it. Wondering what to do. Even got as far as standing at the pharmaceutical section in Boots, staring at the thousand and one types of headache cures. Bought a packet of throat pastels in the end. Ate them all in about an hour, then wondered whether you could overdose on throat pastels. Because that night, I had the dream again. Woke up unable to move, the dream soundtrack still playing in my head.

It was the 'alien' dream but it was different from before. It took me a while to realise why. To focus on the swirling mass of colour that flooded my head, every time I closed my eyes. And with the colours came a memory.

It had been ages since I'd even thought about my 'close encounter'. Sounds a bit odd but once the dreams and the drawing stopped, I forgot all about the alien and the spaceship. Well, maybe not totally. Not at first. But certainly after Melissa's accident. When something like that happens it sort of shoves everything else out of your mind.

But the colours in the dream that night brought it all back.

The screaming alien on the lane. It had been green but it hadn't stayed green. It had started to change colour. Before I fell off my bike I'd definitely seen its colour change, from green to shimmering blue, through to purple. Then later, in my 'lost time', there'd been colours again.

At first the memory wasn't strong. Just the colours. Then, as the dream came back, night after night, I remembered more and I was back on those Internet sites, searching for very special cases. Cases of people who claimed to have been contacted more than once. How did it happen? Could any of them contact aliens at will? How did they do it? What part did dreams play?

It did sort of cross my mind that I was mad. Totally barking, in fact. That I'd simply cracked under all the strain and ought to be signing myself over for psychiatric treatment.

Melissa certainly thought so, once I'd told her my idea.

I wasn't going to tell her until I'd done a bit more research, probed a few more memories in my sleep, but she'd been on at me about the tablets again. And she meant it. She really meant it.

'I'm not getting them,' I told her more definitely than I'd managed before. 'I know a way. A better way.'

'No razors,' she said. 'No knives. I couldn't do that. I couldn't bear it. I'm not brave like that. I can't stand pain.'

'You don't have to have any more pain,' I told her. 'I'm not talking about helping you commit suicide. I'm talking about making you better.'

'My dad's put you up to this, hasn't he?' she said. 'That butcher in America he's found. Well I'm not having any more surgery. I don't want a face like a bloody patchwork quilt, tell him. I'd rather be—'

'This isn't anything to do with your dad,' I said. 'Or surgeons. Listen, Melissa . . . don't shout or scream or interrupt. Just listen. Remember when I told you that story once. About the alien?'

'Don't start all that again, Paul,' she screamed, not even managing to listen for half a second. 'Don't you think my life's bad enough? I don't need this, Paul. I don't want you flipping out on me right now.'

'If it was true,' I insisted. 'If I could prove it to you. If I could prove they helped me . . .'

'Go on then,' she said. 'Show me the implant. Show me the funny little scar under your ear. That's what these X-File freaks have, don't they? Nice how the scars are always so discreet though, don't you think? Not massive great gashes all over their faces. This is a scar, Paul,' she said running her hand along her jaw. 'This is real! Real life, Paul. Not bloody fantasyland.'

'Just let me show you some of the websites,' I tried. 'Some of the other people...'

'Fine,' she said, wheeling herself over to the computer. 'What do I type in? Mental homes? Loony bins? Institutions for the clinically insane?'

'Try alien abduction.'

She did as well. I don't know whether she was trying to humour me, or amuse herself or whether part of her had started to want to believe. Maybe all three.

While she looked, I told her about my own dreams. The more recent ones. The memories they were bringing back.

'Give me a better explanation,' I said, as she laughed. 'Give me a rational explanation for how my eczema cleared up.'

'You grew out of it. People do.'

'In an hour? Bleeding and flaking all over the place one minute. Gone the next. It doesn't make sense.'

'But being cured by colour-changing aliens does, right? And not only did they cure you but they're now going to come back and cure me, yes? Great! What are we waiting for? Open the door. Invite them in.'

'I'm not sure yet,' I confessed. 'I know I'm sort of in touch with them, through the dreams and I've got to the point where I can actually interact. Manipulate the dream. Tell them things. Tell them about you.'

'Fun nights you must have, Paul,' she said, laughing. 'But you were right. You're certainly not alone. There's a woman here who's been abducted seven times. The aliens have helped her come to terms with the fact that her mother twice tried to kill her when she was a child, before handing her over into care where she was abused... Nice, stable psyche we're dealing with here, then, obviously... Ah, yes. She's pregnant herself now. Happened after the last abduction...'

'OK,' I said. 'So some of them sound bit loopy. But I wouldn't discount anything. Not since what happened to me. And besides, some of them are perfectly sane. Let me show you the one about the American Senator.'

'Sure,' said Melissa. 'If he's an American politician he must be sane, mustn't he?'

I showed her all the strongest sites. Hundreds of people with good jobs and otherwise quite normal lives. Not to mention all the evidence from the past. Ancient tribes who drew 'spaceships' and 'aliens' and had knowledge of star systems which they couldn't possibly have worked out for themselves.

'Yeah, yeah,' said Melissa. 'I've heard all that rot before. How aliens built the pyramids and Stonehenge. How the Greek gods were just a pack of fun-loving shape shifters from outer space, having a bit of a wild holiday.'

'Look,' I said, clicking on a picture, making it bigger. 'That looks a bit like the one I saw. Domed head. Only mine didn't have a mouth or feet.'

'Sure,' said Melissa. 'You've told me. You must have seen images like that a thousand times, Paul, on films and games and stuff. It came out of your head. It was never real. It didn't happen.'

But she was wrong. It had happened and it was going to happen again. I was going to make it happen. I was going to make them help Melissa.

Sure, I could understand why she was sceptical. But to me it was all perfectly rational. Perfectly reasonable. I knew they existed. I knew they had cures beyond our understanding. The only question in my mind was how I was going to contact them.

Like I told Melissa, I'd already started to manipulate the dreams. I'd told them what I wanted over and over. 'Lucid dreaming' Melissa called it.

'You might be able to control your dreams, Paul. Some people can,' she said. 'But it's nothing, repeat nothing to do with aliens.'

Was she right? I never actually saw the alien in my dreams. Only the colours. And the aliens never spoke to me. Or did they?

Once the dreams had started again, the drawings started too. When I got home, that night, I pulled all the recent ones out from under the bed. Seascapes. That was it then, wasn't it? It was so glaringly obvious, I was amazed I hadn't seen it before.

Whatever the alien had been doing in that field, land wasn't its natural home. It was a sea-based creature and the sea was where I'd find it again.

The next night, I took Melissa down to the coast. I didn't mention the aliens and Melissa didn't think our seaside excursion odd. We often walked down there, when the weather wasn't too bad. Or too good. If it happened to be a nice night, there might be people around and Melissa wouldn't go.

Of course, we couldn't avoid people altogether on our walks. No matter how late we made it or how foul the weather was, there'd always be someone hanging around. But Melissa always insisted we cross to the other side of the road or that I turned the wheelchair round, so they couldn't see her.

Ridiculous because you couldn't see much anyway. Not with the veil and the waterproof cover which stretched right from her feet up to her chin.

That Thursday night was a bit drizzly. The tide was almost full in but the sea wasn't too rough and we were able to stay by the sea wall, just watching. Well, I guess Melissa was just watching. With me, it was more like waiting. Waiting to see something, feel something.

I didn't and in the end Melissa got fed up, so we moved on.

'Some dream you were having last night, Paul,' Dad said to me over breakfast on Friday morning. 'I came in twice but I didn't like to wake you. You were thrashing around, like you were having a real go at someone. Shouting out.'

'Don't remember,' I said.

But I did. I'd got really good at controlling the dreams.

Remembering them. But I wasn't going to tell Dad that I was shouting at aliens. Telling them they had to help me. Help Melissa.

And I really thought they would. I really believed it. Which is why I wheeled Melissa down there again on Friday night. The weather was worse which was good because it meant there was no one around. Bad because we had to stand well back from the waves crashing over the sea wall and Melissa soon got fed up, though she was way more waterproof than I was.

'Come on, Paul, let's go. I'm freezing.'

'In a minute,' I kept saying.

'What are you doing?' she asked, as I moved round in front of the wheelchair and took my binoculars out of my pocket. 'Bit of a funny time for bird spotting.'

'It's not birds I'm watching, Melissa, look,' I said, suddenly catching a glimpse of something.

'What am I supposed to be looking at?' she asked, taking the binoculars, adjusting them.

'Those lights,' I said. 'Those coloured lights.'

'Boat,' she said, dismissively, handing the binoculars back.

'In this weather!' I said, looking again. 'And it's not just the pinpricks of white and yellow light...it's that red, orange glow on the horizon...'

'Red sky at night,' she quoted. 'Shepherd's delight.'

'It's not a weather phenomenon!' I told her. 'It can't be. Not the way the colours are changing, undulating, like that.'

'Oh yes, silly me!' said Melissa. 'I get it now. It's a spaceship, right? Your alien pals?'

'It could be,' I said. 'I really think it could be.'

'I know you do,' said Melissa, quietly. 'And it scares me, Paul. I'm beginning to think you're more sick than I am. I mean I appreciate how you are with me, what you do for me and all that. But I wonder sometimes, whether it's...normal...Oh, I don't know! I don't know what I'm trying to say. Maybe we're both going crazy. But I sometimes get the feeling that you feel almost responsible, somehow. Like it was somehow your fault. Like you're on some massive guilt trip.'

And she was so close, so near the mark, that I started to cry. Out there, on the promenade sobbing and howling like a five-year-old. And that's how I came to make my next big mistake.

I told her. I told her about seeing, dreaming, wishing her accident, four days before it happened. Waiting, after every word, for the explosion of anger, which never came.

'Oh, Paul!' she said, the minute I'd finished. 'Don't you see? The fantasy bike accident, the alien fantasy, they're both part of the same thing. Your crazy aliens are your way of trying to put it right. Trying to turn back time. Trying to pretend it never happened. But it won't work, Paul. You didn't cause my accident with your fantasy and you can't put it right with one either. Nothing can ever do that.'

I didn't argue. Didn't try to tell her she was right about my guilt hang-up, wrong about my aliens. What was the point? I knew it was only a matter of time before they revealed themselves. Before I had my proof.

What I didn't know was that time had almost run

out. And that on Saturday night, when Melissa eagerly agreed to go down to the coast again, she wasn't planning to indulge me in a bit of alien spotting. She had plans of her own.

We set off, from Melissa's house, at just gone eleven. It was raining but not as heavily as the previous night. We did what I called route C. Along Melissa's road, through the park, round the back of the old canning factory and out onto the coast road. Turning left, towards the muddy, pebbly section of beach which is always empty, even on a hot day in July, let alone a disgusting January night.

Once, before people started jetting off abroad for their holidays, our little bit of coast was quite popular. Pre-war tourists presumably didn't mind the mud, quicksand, rocks, hidden channels, dangerous tides and buckets of rain which make it a little less popular these days.

There are still signs of the old tourist boom. The half dozen or so gift shops in town, struggling to keep going. Two massive hotels, one still trading, the other turned into flats. The odd boarded-up beach hut or ruined café set back amongst the trees and overgrown bushes.

'Remember the old café?' said Melissa as we paused by the sea wall.

I think I must have nodded.

'I'd like to go there,' she said.

'Why? What for?' I asked, gazing out to sea. 'We'd probably never be able to find it, in the dark.'

'Neither would anyone else, that's the point,' said Melissa. 'And I've brought a torch.'

She unzipped the waterproof covering, slightly, to reveal a carrier bag tucked underneath. Opened the top of the bag. Took out a torch. Shone it on the rest of the bag's contents. Just for a second. Just long enough for me to see.

'Melissa! No! How did you . . . where did you get it all?'

'I told you,' she said. 'I've been saving up the tablets for ages. The bottled water's kept where I can reach it and the whisky and vodka I got by wedging myself up against the settee and raiding the drinks cabinet. Bit tricky that! Nearly brought the whole bloody lot down on top of me. But I managed and there's so much in there, they'll never miss a bottle or six.'

'No!' I said again.

'Why not? You don't have to do anything. Just take me somewhere quiet and leave me. Or you could stay. . .'

'No!'

'It's no use staring out to sea, Paul,' she said, her laughter high-pitched, hysterical. 'There's only one way to make it all better. Only one way to make the pain go away.'

She stopped laughing and stared at me, her eyes shining incredibly blue, even in the darkness.

'Think about it, Paul. One last little party. One lovely, long, peaceful sleep.'

I put my hands on the wheelchair to turn it round. Take her home.

'No point, Paul,' she said, laughing again. 'I'll do it one day. With or without your help. You know that, don't you?

And you'll always feel guilty, won't you? You'll always believe it was your fault. But you don't have to feel guilty. You could come with me . . .'

Was she saying what I thought she was saying? Come with me as in take the tablets? Take a chance on the afterlife? Well, a bit stressed I might have been. A bit unhinged even. But suicidal I wasn't.

So why didn't I finish turning the wheelchair? Why didn't I take her straight home? Why did I wheel her towards the ramp?

We definitely went down the ramp. I remember because it was no easy business. The ramp down to the beach is a relic of the old tourist boom days too. Bit of a death trap in itself with its bumps and holes where planks used to be but we made it, poor Melissa almost flying out of the chair as we crash-landed on the beach.

'We won't be able to get the wheelchair over the rocks,' she said. 'You'll have to carry me.'

She thought I was going to take her to the café. She really thought that. But I wasn't, was I? I wasn't ever going to do that. So what WAS I doing?

It wasn't exactly inviting, down there. Pitch black apart from the barely noticeable flicker of lights in the distance. Tide coming in fast. But not so wild and angry like the night before.

I remember unzipping the waterproof covering, lifting Melissa out of the wheelchair. Telling her to put the bag down. It was too heavy.

'We don't need that,' I said.

But she wouldn't let go of it.

'Where are we going?' she said. 'Not that way, Paul. Over there. Across the rocks.'

'I know what I'm doing,' I said.

But did I? Moving towards the lights. Drawn towards the sea like I was walking in my sleep. So certain that it would be all right. But was it? It can't have been because I can't remember what happened next. The memories won't come.

Lights. That's all I can see. That's all I remember. That and the sound of the waves and Melissa screaming.

Why can't I remember? What happened next? Where did we go? What did I do? Why was she screaming? What am I trying to hide?

Chapter 12

PAUL

It's coming back! I can see it now. All of it. Most of it. Some
of it. The iceberg's melted and a great rush of water is
sweeping all the memories to the front of my mind. Or is
the rush of water the sea? Is that what I can hear? The
sudden wave that crashed over us, huge and terrifying.

That and the sound of Melissa still screaming.

Only suddenly there's no water, no waves, no sea. And
I'm lying on a sort of cloud, all transparent and squidgy.
Very soft. Relaxing. Peaceful. Calm. The sort of death
they used to imagine in the old days. And I remember
thinking that I hadn't thought death would be like this.
So instant. One minute thrashing around, the breath
being crushed out of you and the next...

'Get them away from me,' Melissa yells right into my
left ear, breaking the spell. 'I hate spiders. I hate spiders.'

Not dead then, maybe. Not if I can hear the yelling and
feel Melissa's sharp, long nails, tearing gashes down my arm.

And the calmness I feel seeping through our cloud-
cushion isn't getting to Melissa at all. She stops ripping my
arm but only to grab my head, wrenching it round. 180
degrees, it feels like, and suddenly I see them too. Her
spiders.

Two of them. Grey. Blubbery, bulbous bodies. Size of large dogs. Tangle of grey legs spreading out all over the place. But they're backing away. As though they're terrified.

So, a dream then? Hallucination? The very moment of death?

But it's hard to think. Hard to focus. Because, all the time, Melissa's scratching, biting, ripping, tearing, trying to hurl herself off our cushion which somehow holds us fast.

As the creatures back off, their skin starts to shimmer, grey, yellow, green, blue, purple, pink. A kaleidoscope of colours blending, forming patterns, calming and hypnotic. And as I watch, I begin to understand.

It happened. It's happening. I was right. They came. They rescued us. They're here to help.

Melissa must sense something too because she's stopped screaming and clawing.

'They're not spiders, Melissa,' I tell her. 'They're not spiders. They won't hurt you.'

I know it's true but I don't know why it's true. Then something else happens.

The smaller one pulls itself upright. Four of the limbs go into the side, merging with the now dark green body. Only four limbs showing now. The two it stands on and the other two waving at its side.

And what had seemed like one huge body sort of separates into body and head with eyes on top, making it look, not exactly human but humanoid, like my green kid on the lane.

111

'They're changing shape,' Melissa hisses. 'What are they? What the hell are they?'

Octopus. That's what they're like. The trademark of my drawings. Real octopus change shape and colour. I've seen it on a wild life programme once. The octopus that goes brown and bumpy, like a rock. One that streamlines to mimic a fish. OK, not so dramatic as this but enough to make me believe it's possible. This is all real.

The floor I can see through my cloud cushion – like the sea-bed only without the sea. And all around us, a smallish cave-shaped structure. Made of the same clear, wobbly jelly as our cloud. Clear, transparent, I think, but there's nothing outside or else everything outside is total blackness.

'What are they doing?' Melissa screams as the two creatures edge forward. 'Get me out of here, Paul.'

Before I have a chance to move, a tentacle whips out towards us, so fast that I gasp and almost choke. But it wasn't aiming it at us. It was aiming at the cushion. Piercing it. Injecting it. Flooding it with vivid rainbow colours which spill over us.

No, not over us. Through us. I can feel the colours washing through my body and my mind and each colour tastes, feels, smells different. And if this isn't crazy enough, I have the weirdest feeling that it's all happened before.

'P...a...u...l,' Melissa says, her voice sounding as though it had been slowed down. 'I feel so...so...strange, floaty...I'm scared, Paul.'

But the hysteria in her voice has gone, her eyes are closed and she doesn't really sound scared anymore. The two aliens are still colour shimmering but I can feel they're relaxed now, too.

'Calmer now, good.'

I hear the voice in my head. It isn't coming from anywhere but I know it must be.

'Did you hear that?' I ask Melissa.

'Music,' she says. 'I can hear music. Like whale song.'

'She may be able to understand soon. Give her more time,' the voice in my head tells me, washed along by the colours.

The colours. The colours are the key. See how the colours on the creatures become the colours on the cushion become the colours in my head. And it's all so obvious now!

'Open your eyes, Melissa.'

'Why?' she asks, sort of distant and dreamy.

'So you can hear them.'

'What?' she says, like she's not really with me at all.

'Open your eyes,' I tell her. 'And you'll see. You listen with your eyes!'

'That's silly,' she says, all giggly, like she was drunk or something.

And suddenly we're both laughing together. Feeling so unbelievably, euphorically, amazingly happy.

'Too powerful,' says the voice in my head, as the colours start to fade.

'Are they hurt?' says another voice, as the colours settle, a little less strongly now.

'I don't think so. But they could have been. You should never have brought them . . .'

'I'm sorry. But what was I to do? When they walked right out into the sea like that. And the female so damaged as she is.'

'You could have left them.'

'But don't you see what this means? The boy child. It's the same one we helped. He's come back to us. He remembered us! His mind must be far more advanced than we thought. He's remembered and he's brought his injured friend.'

'Far better he forgot. This could ruin everything.'

'Tell me this isn't happening,' Melissa says and I know she can see the voices too.

'She's frightened!'

I experiment. I close my eyes. And there are no more voices until I open them again.

'Look,' says a voice. 'He understands! I really think these creatures are less primitive and savage than we thought.'

'I don't know. Best to be careful. Don't get too close.'

'We took the tablets, didn't we?' said Melissa, suddenly. 'That's it, isn't it? These are hallucinations, aren't they, Paul?'

'So sad!' comes the voice. 'She wanted to kill herself. But you're safe now. We can help you.'

'No we can't, Torflin! We must take them back.'

'No,' I shout out.

They both leap backwards.

'Please,' I see them say. 'It hurts us when you do that. Your thought waves are strong enough.'

'You read minds?' I say in my head.

114

'In a sense, yes. As can you, if we enhance the colours, you see.'

Did I see? I wasn't sure. It didn't matter. Only one thing mattered.

'Yes.'

The reply came almost before I realised I'd thought the thought.

'To repair the damage to your friend would be easy enough.'

'This is crazy,' says Melissa, shaking her head. 'Like they're answering questions we haven't asked.'

'Sssh,' I tell her. 'Our voices hurt them. You just think the questions.'

'Yes,' says a voice, obviously responding to whatever Melissa had just thought.

'Your friend has been with us before. I'd been collecting a few cell samples from land mammals – sheep...'

And the voice takes me back to that day on the lane. Only I'm seeing it through their eyes, not mine. The poor injured creature lying on the lane next to its primitive vehicle. Leave it. Far safer to leave it. Humans can be dangerous. They're not like sheep.

But it doesn't seem dangerous. It's not moving. Might even be dead. Feels warm. Not dead. But it might die, if we leave it. It couldn't harm, just to take a look. As long as we keep it asleep. Could be useful for research.

Such a fragile body. Was all that damage from one little accident? All those sores. Almost blind, poor thing. Arm bone snapped. Best to repair everything. Put it back

115

where we found it. It won't remember. It won't understand. It won't ever know.

'This is amazing!' whispers Melissa, sounding for the first time since the accident, like the old Melissa. 'This is like, so, so amazing! I'm seeing what they see. Feeling what they feel. I'm talking to aliens! Amphibious aliens. I bet I'm the first person on earth ever to have made contact! Me! They're talking to me!'

'Er... and me,' I point out, not even knowing whether we're both hearing and seeing the same things.

'Well, yes you, obviously.'

'And what about all those people we read about on the Net?'

'They were just nutters,' Melissa says, dismissively. 'But this is real. Really happening. Imagine, Paul, aliens living right off our coastline and nobody knew!'

She tries to pull herself up, like she's forgotten all about her injuries, her paralysis. Even when she flops back, she doesn't get angry or frustrated.

'I want to touch them,' she says.

This from the girl who'd been one large hysterical scream, only minutes before.

They don't look too keen but the slightly smaller one, who is Torflin, I think, stretches a tentative tentacle.

'Wow!' says Melissa, shuddering, as he makes contact. 'Amazing.'

And I feel Melissa pleading, begging, followed by a sort of musical laughter in my head. Hers? Theirs? Mine?

'Yes, yes, we can do it. We WILL do it. If you're sure.'

And I know what she's asked them because I can feel everything, see everything, hear everything as though all my senses are about a million times sharper than before.

'You'll be able to walk again, yes. And your face? Yes, that too. But you must be sure. You must understand . . .'

'Did you hear that?' Melissa whispers. 'I'm going to be well again, Paul. I'm going to be well!'

'Of course you can trust us,' says a voice full of hurt.

And I know they've read a thought I didn't mean to think.

'There will be conditions, of course.'

Melissa keeps nodding as they speak. Agreeing to everything.

But I'm not sure. It's all moving so fast. And I'm hearing replies, questions, everybody's thoughts all at once. With my own still battling to get through, trying to make sense of it all, if there's any sense to be found. It's all too much, these new, powerful feelings are drowning me, swallowing me. So I'm not sure exactly what she's agreeing to. My brain's starting to feel detached, confused, my stomach's churning up and I think I'm going to be sick.

Maybe it's because our cushion's moving. Separating. Pushed by a tentacle. My half floats off a little to the right but Melissa's closes round her like a ball. She's huddled up inside and it reminds me of some pictures Mum showed me of Jenna curled up in the womb before she was ever born.

'Stay calm,' the colours say but they're talking to Melissa, not me. 'Once the gel fully closes, you won't feel a thing, I promise.'

117

I pull myself up a bit, waiting, watching, as the bigger creature, presses up close to Melissa's ball, like he was part of it. Pushing a tentacle inside, making contact with Melissa.

'This isn't happening,' I tell myself. 'It isn't real.'

'It's all right,' says the smaller one, Torflin, as the ball starts to flood with colours, so strong, I have to turn away, looking at Torflin's paler colours instead. 'Don't you remember?'

I shake my head. Was this what had happened to me? Had I been wrapped in a ball of gel while tentacles prodded and probed? Is that what they did to me that day on the lane?

'Yes.'

So I knew what they'd done and in part why they'd done it. But there were still millions of questions left unanswered. Who were they? What were they doing here? Where did they come from? What did they want from us? How had they rescued us from the sea? HAD they rescued us? Was this even happening at all?

The creatures seemed real enough but the detached voices? The gel cushion? The sheer impossibility of it all?

'All this is tiring you,' was the only reply. 'You must sleep.'

I don't want to sleep. I mustn't fall asleep. Must stay awake. But I can't. The cushion's closing around me. I can't move. I can't fight it. My limbs feel heavy, frozen. I can't see, I can't hear, I can't feel, I can't breathe.

Chapter 13

PAUL

How long was I in that gel bubble? I don't know. Days rather than hours, I think. Days of lost time, lost consciousness. When anything could have happened.

But the good news is, I didn't do anything stupid or criminal, did I? I didn't help Melissa to...do what she wanted to do. The bad news is, that the real story is just a touch weird.

Even lying here telling it quietly to myself, I know how crazy it sounds. And if I tried to tell anyone else?

Maybe if Melissa tells the same story. But she won't. She can't. She's not here. Because it all went wrong, didn't it?

I remember my gel bubble opening. And it wasn't like coming out from an anaesthetic all groggy or anything, more like waking from a deep, refreshing sleep.

I can see Torflin and the other one whose name was Krespron. At least, that's what the names sounded like to me. And there's Melissa still curled up in her gel ball. But the colours are white/grey muted and, for a moment that's how they stay. Pale and silent. And I know there's been some dreadful mistake. She's not moving. There's no colour, no life.

'Melissa!' I shout out.

I can't help it. I know it hurts them but I can't help it. I have to bite my lip to stop myself screaming. Close my eyes, to squeeze back the tears. It's my fault. I shouldn't have done it. I shouldn't have brought her here.

'Paul!'

Melissa's voice, quiet but bright, alert, squelchy.

No. The squelchy is something else. My eyes snap open and I see Melissa bouncing up and down on her opened cushion like a crazy four-year-old on a bouncy castle.

'Look!' she whispers, touching her face, as she bounces. 'Does it look like it feels, Paul? Does it look like me?'

And I can't speak. She looks so good. So perfect. If anything, more perfect than before.

'There is no need to thank us,' comes a shimmering pink through to orange voice. 'For us, these things are easy enough.'

It's Melissa who's thanked them, not me. And I feel guilty because all I'm really thinking about is how long I might have been here and how much I want to go home. And I understand, for the first time, homesickness because that's what it feels like. A sickness. A real desperation to be back in the real world. To touch normality.

'Home?' I see Torflin say.

'Yes. It's just that it must have been . . . it feels like a long time.'

'I told you, Torflin,' says the other voice. 'I told you how it would be. They can't survive in our environment even for a few days!'

'But when we build them gel-suits? When they can swim around with us?'

'It's not only a physical problem, Torflin. It's psychological, social, cultural. See the strength of its feelings! See how its mind floats from one reality to another, not being able to anchor in either.'

'But they understood all that,' said Torflin. 'They knew.'

'Wait a minute,' I said, trying not to speak aloud. 'Knew what?'

But I realised, even as I said it, that I was fooling myself. Playing some sort of game.

The conditions.

The conditions I'd tried to ignore. Tried to pretend weren't real. Somewhere in the time when I'd half hoped, half believed that none of this was real. While the other half of me had been so desperate to believe they could make Melissa well, I'd have agreed to anything.

Even this. The price of Melissa's healing. That we would never go home. I knew it. I'd heard it. I'd felt it.

'You do see, don't you? We have to protect ourselves. How could you possibly explain Melissa's recovery, if we let you go back? What would you tell people?'

So there it was. So obvious really. Explaining away my eczema and short-sight had been easy-peasy. But how could we explain this? 'Er...Melissa fell out of her wheelchair, got a nasty bump on the head and suddenly she could walk again. Oh, and yes...all the scar tissue disappeared as well.'

'And if we tell the truth?'

121

'Impossible!' comes the reply. 'It would be a disaster, for us, for your species, beyond imagining. The time is not right.'

They don't explain but I can feel it's true.

'But if we stayed here for a while,' I try, knowing how feeble my argument sounds. 'And then said Melissa got her treatment abroad, somewhere?'

No answer. Probably because my thoughts are crowding in, spinning round, confusing them as well as me.

'He's already under great stress. I knew how it would be. Much more of this and his mind will be ripped apart. There is only one solution. We must send you back exactly as you were. As though none of this had ever happened.'

'Wait a minute?' says Melissa, voicing her thoughts. 'What do you mean? Exactly as we were?'

'Reverse the operation.'

And I know what she's thinking. I know what she's screaming in her head because they start cajoling, reasoning.

'We're sorry. We are really sorry. But it's the only way. You won't feel pain, Melissa, and if it is possible to make minor repairs to make you more comfortable, without being noticeable, then we will. We do not mean to be cruel. We do not wish you to suffer. But if you stay here, you will. Far more than we realised.'

'This is your fault,' Melissa hisses at me. 'Tell them, Paul. Tell them you'll be OK. This is just shock, panic. Once you get used to the idea, you'll be fine. We'll both be fine. Tell them!'

But I can't. I know I can't stay. I know I can't give up my life, my real life. I can't stay floating in this wilderness, not being able to connect with anything. I can't do it. Not even for Melissa.

'Wait, wait, wait,' comes the voice of Torflin. 'Two strong voices, each saying different. What if Melissa were to stay alone?'

I know she's agreed. Instantly. Immediately. She doesn't say it aloud. She doesn't have to.

'What about your parents, Melissa?' I whisper. 'Family. Friends. How will they feel? When you don't come back? When you don't ever come back?'

'How would they feel, Paul, if I did? You know what it was like. You know why you brought me here. They'll be hurt. I know that. But not as much as I'd hurt them if I went back. Thinking I was dead would be easier for them in the end. Easier than trying to live with me as I was.'

'That isn't true,' I say, but I think perhaps it is.

'So sad,' says a colour voice. 'So very sad.'

'Melissa,' I plead. 'Think about it. What's going to happen once the high of being well again wears off? When you start thinking about friends and family? When you start missing them?'

'I miss them already,' says Melissa. 'I always will. But I can cope with that. Better than I could cope with being a freak, a cripple.'

'You don't know that. You don't know how you'll feel week after week. Month after month. You'll hate this. You'll hate being alone. I know you will.'

'Then stay with me.'

But I can't. I can't. I can't.

'It's all right, Paul,' says Melissa. 'I understand. And I won't be alone, will I?'

She looks at the creatures and I try to hide the thoughts that come.

'It's all right. You can think it. We're aliens. We're different. And we already know how difficult you humans find it to live with those who are different. You can't even live in peace with those of your own species who have a different culture, colour or creed.'

They're making us sound like bigots, racists! And I guess Melissa takes offence too, because it's her they answer.

'Maybe the colour doesn't matter to you, Melissa. Or even the fact that we have eight limbs. Maybe you'd even get used to our customs, in time. But the real problem is our environment. We live in water most of the time. At great depths. Here. And on our home world. If you stayed with us you'd always be caged in your suit, your bubble, your cave. You'd never be totally free, would you?'

But she tells them she wasn't free before. Stuck in that chair. Hiding her face behind a veil.

She doesn't say it but I've started to feel her thoughts, like she's part of me, like we're all part of each other. And that's how I remember the conversations. Like it's all taking place in my head, out of my head, at the same time. All the voice parts mingling, like a choir, so it's hard to separate them.

'We think,' the Krespron part says, 'that it was a prison you built for yourself…but if you think you would be happier with us, then so be it.'

And Melissa's smiling. As if we're planning a nice little holiday for her. And I'm not at all sure she knows what she's doing. But there's no way I'm going to change her mind. Or mine.

Changing my mind. Now, there's a thought. Because that was another condition, wasn't it? Of me coming back? It had to be, didn't it? Because there was no way they could let me come back knowing what I knew.

There're more conversations, more sounds, more colours but it's all too mixed up. I can't sort it out. It won't unravel. But I know they did something. Something in my head. I'm left with an image of deep grey with one sharp blast of red as the gel bubble closes around me again.

I think I said something to Melissa first. I think she answered me. But I don't get any words. Only a feeling. That it would all be all right.

But it's not all right, is it? When I lost consciousness…whatever they did to me then didn't work, did it? Because when I found myself staggering up the beach in the pouring rain, I had a massive iceberg where my brain used to be.

And now. Now that the iceberg's finally started to melt, what am I left with? How do I know how much of this is true and how much is implanted? For all I know they could have killed Melissa and implanted a memory that she was fine and happy.

Or these might not be memories at all. They might be pure fantasy. Madness. An extension of the madness that set in when I fell off my bike that day.

One thing's for sure, nothing's working out like it was supposed to. There was supposed to be a memory, I think. Wasn't that what they tried to do? Make me remember a story. A story that would explain it all?

So maybe that's the way forward. Maybe that's what I should do. Try to remember the story. Or make up a story myself. Something that won't make it any harder for Melissa's parents. Something that won't get me into trouble. Melissa being swept out to sea perhaps? Me trying to rescue her?

Will they buy that? Can I do it? Can I fix a lie in my mind which I'll be able to stick to under questioning, under hypnosis? A lie I'll have to live with forever?

Or should I let my brain freeze over again? Freeze so hard it will never thaw. So much easier that way. Won't have to talk. Won't have to think. Won't have to explain. Won't have to ask myself over and over whether all this is real. Whether I did the right thing. Won't even have to remember.

Just let the gel take hold again. That's what it is. Gel, not ice. Only it won't freeze. My brain's completely free now and by the look on Laura's face I think my tongue might be too. I think I might have been talking just then.

Chapter 14

Laura was leaning so far forward, her face was almost touching Paul's and she hardly dared breathe. He'd been talking. Soft, incoherent rambling, so Laura could barely tell whether he was awake or asleep.

She pulled back, slightly, as his eyes opened fully, to allow him some space.

'Paul?' she said.

'Hi.'

One word spoken calmly and directly. One word which made her want to stand up, rush around the room cheering and waving her arms.

She reached for the bell press.

'No,' Paul said.

'We ought to get the doctor,' said Laura.

'No,' Paul said again. 'Not yet. I want to get used to it first. Being back. It feels strange.'

'I nearly got the nurse in before,' said Laura. 'You were muttering. Sort of half asleep.'

'What did I say?'

'Not much that made sense,' said Laura, smiling. 'But you kept saying a name.'

'Melissa?'

Laura nodded.

'She's still missing,' Laura said, gently.

Paul's turn to nod.

'You know that?' said Laura, shivering. 'You know she's still missing.'

'She isn't coming back,' said Paul, speaking slowly, battling to stop the words which kept spilling out. 'She isn't ever coming back. And it's my fault. I thought I could help her. But it all went wrong. She can't come back. And now I don't know what to do, what to say, how to explain. You've got to help me, Laura. You've got to help me.'

'Sssh,' said Laura, looking round at the nurse who had come into the room, in her soft, soundless shoes.

How long had she'd been there? What had she heard?

'He's still sick,' Laura said. 'He's been rambling. He doesn't know what he's saying.'

'I'll get the doctor and your parents,' the nurse said.

'It was an accident, wasn't it, Paul?' Laura urged. 'Whatever happened to Melissa was an accident, wasn't it?'

'No,' said Paul. 'Not really. It's all gone wrong. I tried to help. I wanted to help her.'

'What are you telling me?' whispered Laura. 'That you helped her...to die?'

'No,' Paul shouted. 'Not that. I wouldn't do that! She's not dead. She's alive.'

'Alive?' said Laura. 'But you said...I thought...I mean...alive? That's brilliant! Where is she? Just tell me where she was when you left her.'

'I can't! I don't know. I'm not supposed to say...I...'

'Well you're going to have to,' said Laura. 'I don't care what she made you promise. Or where she's trying to hide herself away. You have to tell. Because if you don't, Paul, you're going to be up on some sort of murder charge.'

'It's not that easy. She's alive. She's fine but they won't be able to find her. They won't believe me.'

'I will,' said Laura. 'You know I will. Tell me. Tell me now. Whatever it is, I'll believe you. I promise. You know I will.'

Paul laughed. A strange, hysterical sound that didn't sound like Paul at all.

'OK,' said Paul. 'Try this. Melissa's with aliens. She's alive. She's beautiful again. She can walk. They made her better. But they don't want anyone to know about them. So Melissa's chosen to stay. Under the sea. That's why she isn't coming back.'

'Oh, Paul!'

Laura had thought the words but it was someone else who screamed them. It was her mother, coming into the room, closely followed by Dad, Dr Kapra and Dr Corrigan.

Laura stood up and moved away from the bed as the others swarmed round. She walked over to the window for a breath of air but it was closed and she couldn't summon the energy to open it. She felt a sudden, overwhelming sickness and slumped to the floor.

She was vaguely aware of someone lifting her but didn't know who. Perhaps her dad, who was the first person she saw when she opened her eyes.

'I'm sorry,' she said.

'Sorry?' said her dad, helping her to sit up. 'What are you apologising for?'

Laura sipped the drink he offered her and looked round, before answering. She was lying on a bed, right at the end of the main ward.

'Fainting like that,' Laura said. 'As if you haven't got enough problems. As if you and Mum haven't got enough to worry about. How is he? Where's Paul?'

'He's still in his room. And, thanks to you, he's talking again. So you certainly don't need to apologise.'

'I don't think it was anything to do with me,' said Laura. 'Besides, he's not exactly talking sense, is he?'

'Not when I left, no,' said her dad. 'But he will. He's traumatised, at the moment. Confused. But Dr Kapra's confident that once he's talked out his fantasies, she'll be able to get at what's behind them.'

'You can go back, if you like,' said Laura. 'I'm fine now.'

'No I'll . . .'

'I'd like you to,' said Laura. 'I want to know what's happening.'

When her dad popped back, an hour or so later, it wasn't good news. Paul's story was getting weirder by the minute. He was claiming he'd met the aliens before.

'Not hard to guess where that's coming from, is it?' said Laura. 'It's the story Melissa put round about the abduction. About the aliens curing his eczema!'

'In a sense,' said her dad, 'it doesn't really matter where the fantasy is coming from, does it? The point is, he's

130

using it to cover something. Something so terrible that he's gone into complete denial. The police think...'

'The police?' said Laura.

'They've been listening to the hypnosis tapes again and the doctor has finally let them have a word with Paul.'

Laura opened her mouth to protest but her dad stopped her.

'It's Saturday, Laura,' he said. 'A full week since they went missing. If there's any chance of finding Melissa, any chance of finding her alive, then it has to be soon.'

'Dad,' said Laura slowly. 'What'll happen? What'll happen if they don't ever find her? What'll happen to Paul?'

Her dad shook his head.

'It'll be all right,' he said. 'Nothing will happen.'

'This is me you're talking to, Dad! Laura. Not Jenna. You don't have to pretend. You don't have to protect me.'

'Maybe it's myself I'm protecting, love,' he said. 'Maybe I don't want to face it any more than you do. I think we both know how bad it looks. And however much we love Paul, however much we believe in him... what he's been saying in there, what he said to you, earlier, virtually amounts to a confession.'

'Does it?' said Laura. 'Let's say we took it all at face value. Lets say we took everything he's said as truth. The aliens. Everything.'

'If we do that,' said her dad. 'If we believe that Paul is telling the truth as he sees it, then that leads us down a different route. And I'm not sure it's a better one.'

'I don't mean the truth as he sees it,' said Laura. 'I'm

131

not suggesting that we shrug our shoulders and accept that he's mad.'

'So what are you suggesting?'

'That I do what I promised I'd do. That I let myself believe him, however bizarre it sounds. Do you remember that book you used to read me when I was little – *The Lion, the Witch and the Wardrobe*?'

'Sort of. Yes. Why?'

'Because I read it to Jenna recently. Do you remember the part where Lucy and Edward have both been into the wardrobe, both seen the land of Narnia? Only Edward denies it, doesn't he?'

'I don't know. I'm not sure. I don't see where this is leading.'

'The two older children, Susan and Peter,' said Laura, 'go to see The Professor because they're worried about what they see as Lucy's fantasies. And The Professor asks them who they think is the more truthful, Lucy or Edward.'

'And they agree it's Lucy,' said her dad. 'I remember now. And it turns out that Lucy has been telling the truth all along. There really is another world, through the wardrobe. But that's fiction, Laura. It's a story. Magical lions, wicked witches and aliens happen in stories. It's where they belong.'

'You're missing the point,' said Laura.

'If the point is whether Paul is always truthful,' said her dad, 'then I'm afraid the answer is no. He's no more truthful than anyone else under pressure. Did he admit to breaking my greenhouse window? No. He tried to tell me a bird must have flown into it, even when I found his cricket ball in the middle of my tomato plants. Did he tell me when he got sacked from his paper round? No. He carried on going out at half past five for a fortnight before we found out. Paul lies, Jenna lies, you lie. We all do, Laura.'

'OK,' said Laura. 'So he tells white lies. But they're all pretty straightforward, aren't they? Not great, complicated stories like this. Paul never even played fantasy games like me and Jenna. He couldn't. He never had that sort of imagination.'

'He plays video games,' said her dad. 'Sci-fi games. He watches TV, films. *Star Trek*, *Star Wars*, *The X-Files*, *Men in Black*. He's seen them all. And if he was going to make up a fantasy of any kind, I reckon aliens is what it would be. I'm not saying this is on a conscious level, Laura. It's a breakdown of some sort, the doctors say.'

'It's not a breakdown,' said Laura. 'I know how crazy the alien stuff sounds but he's not the only one to have seen something, is he? What about the huge 'flying fish' Cider Joe said he saw? Wouldn't that tie in?'

Her dad's look, the raised eyebrow told her how much credibility Joe's statements were likely to get.

'Laura,' said her dad, squeezing her hand, 'I'd like to let myself believe in the aliens too. That way I could believe that Paul isn't mentally ill and he hasn't done anything terrible. But don't you see? That's why Paul has invented them. They're his shield. His protection. And I just don't think it would help if we start hiding behind them too.'

Chapter 15

Rolling colours. Voices carried on ripples of light. Four voices. One mind.

'Paul? Can you hear me? We're with you. We're still with you.'

'Why? Why can't you just let me go?'

'We need to bring you back. Can you hear what I'm saying? You need to come back to us.'

'No. Not now. I'm home now.'

'Not really. You're neither in one reality or the other. It's dangerous, Paul. Dangerous for us. Dangerous for you. The panic. The confusion. You can't handle it. How many times have you changed your story, Paul? Melissa drowned. Melissa may have taken an overdose. Melissa's with aliens. They're not going to believe you, Paul. They're not going to believe any of it, in the end. They'll say you're mad. They'll lock you away.'

'No! I can tell them. I can explain. I can make them understand!'

'They'll never understand. You don't even understand it yourself. You don't know what's true anymore. Come back. Stay with us. With Melissa.'

Tempting voices which taste of chocolate. Visions of Melissa perfect and happy. No more problems. No more explanations. Leave it all behind. Go back to them. Forget about Laura, Jenna, my parents, my friends, my life . . .

Melissa's voice detaches itself from the rest.

'No, he can't do that. I don't want him to do that. It isn't fair. Listen to me. There's a way. Another way.'

'No!' Paul shouted as he woke.

He'd managed to open his eyes but, for the moment couldn't move anything else. Was it the pills they'd given him making his body feel so heavy and aching? Or was it the dream? Such a strange dream. Not vague, like the others. A drama unfolding in his head. Krespron, Torflin and Melissa. Talking amongst themselves. Talking to him. Talking about him. Talking through him. Telling him something. Something important. Something he had to do. Then Melissa had said, had thought . . .

'No,' Paul said again, pulling himself up into a sitting position.

He could tell by the muted lighting that it was late. He made his eyes focus on the clock on the wall. Five past eleven.

The little camp bed they'd set up for Mum was empty. If he could just move before his mother came back . . . get down to the sea . . . that was where he had to go, wasn't it?

If only he could find the energy. All he wanted to do was sleep but he couldn't. The dream voices were still there. Melissa's the strongest.

'There's a way out of this. Another way.'

It was the prompt he needed. Paul got out of bed,

moved towards the door, slipped out onto the empty corridor and turned left, towards the exit sign. Halfway along the corridor he stopped, looking down at his bare feet and legs. What was he thinking of? How far did he think he was going to get only half dressed?

He turned and headed back to his room, searching in the locker for a sweatshirt and trousers to put on over his pyjamas. Some socks. A pair of shoes. He dressed as quickly as he could, certain that his mother would return at any moment.

His legs felt sore and heavy, as he headed along the corridor once more. As though his body simply wasn't interested in going where his mind told him he must. He wasn't even quite sure where that was. Only that he had to leave the hospital unnoticed.

Despite his tiredness he used the stairs in preference to the lift. Less chance of being seen. The tricky bit, he knew, would be going through the entrance foyer, past the main reception desk. But luck was on his side. An ambulance had just drawn up outside and someone was being wheeled through on a stretcher, drawing everyone's attention.

Paul summoned all his energy and walked, briskly, confidently, through the main doors as a blast of cold air rushed to greet him.

He hurried on, as fast as he could. Partly because moving fast would be protection against the cold and partly because he knew it was a long walk from the hospital to the coast.

No doubt now, in his mind, where he was going. But what was he going to do when he got there? Walk into the sea again? Go back? So Melissa could stay.

Wasn't that the choice now? Wasn't that what the dream meant? Hadn't that always been the choice? He had to go back to their reality or Melissa had to come back to his, with all its scars and pain and agony.

He couldn't be sure. Couldn't think straight. Because all the time the dream voices played in his head and with them the curious, sceptical, questioning voices of the doctors and the police.

'So you're saying now that Melissa might have taken some sort of overdose before you ever left her house on Saturday?'

'And that a girl who was already doped up on something propelled her wheelchair into the sea. And you couldn't stop her?'

'Oh, I see. You didn't want to stop her because you knew the aliens would be there. We're back to them again, are we?'

'No! Yes! It's the truth!'

Paul's own voice startled him. He'd shouted the words out loud. He paused. Leant for a moment against someone's gate. Looked round, anxiously, with the uneasy feeling that he was being followed.

Paranoia, he told himself. There was no one there. A dozen or so parked cars. A ginger cat crossing the narrow street. Otherwise nothing. Was this madness? Was this what it felt like to be crazy? Hunted, haunted, confused.

He moved on but as he did so the feeling came again. Someone was watching him. Someone was definitely watching.

Laura cursed as her mobile rang. She checked the caller and decided she couldn't ignore it. She stopped the car.

'Laura?' her dad's voice said. 'Where are you? Your mum said you left the hospital ages ago. She's just phoned. Paul's disappeared. He's not in his room. They've searched the hospital. They can't find—'

'I know,' said Laura. 'I spotted him as he was leaving the hospital. I've been following him.'

'Following him? Laura, where is he? What's he doing? Why didn't you phone?'

'I don't know. I was going to. I haven't had time. I didn't want to lose sight of him. And now I have. I should be able to pick him up again, though. I think he's heading for the coast.'

'All right. Tell me where you are now. I'll phone the police and then I'll come straight down.'

'Not the police.'

'Laura we have to. Who knows what he'll try to do, the state he's in. Now where are you?'

Laura told him, checked her mirror and pulled out from the kerb. There was no sign of Paul but she knew she had to find him. Find him before anyone else did. She should have stopped him. Stopped him earlier. Just pulled up beside him and made him get into the car.

Why hadn't she? Because he'd seemed, somehow, so

purposeful. As if he knew where he was going. As if he might be able to lead her to the truth.

Out on the coast road, she saw him again. Standing by the sea wall. She saw something else too. A police car parked by 'The Marine View' hotel. She pulled in behind them as two policemen got out. She recognised them both. The older one because he'd interviewed her when Paul went missing. The younger one because it was Carl Hodges, an ex-boyfriend from school days.

'Wait,' she hissed at them. 'You'll frighten him. Let me go.'

Suddenly Paul cried out. Loud enough for them to hear quite clearly.

'It's too late. It's too late. Melissa, no!'

As he cried out, he rushed down the steps, onto the beach.

'There's another car and an ambulance on its way,' Carl told Laura, as all three of them raced across the road and stood by the wall, looking down on Paul.

'Where's he going? What's he doing?' the older policeman whispered, as they watched Paul, keeping close to the wall, making his way to the left, starting to clamber up some rocks and into the bushes beyond.

'I think we need to stop him, now,' said Carl. 'Before he does himself any damage.'

'Just give it a minute,' said the other man. 'You never know. He might lead us to something.'

Laura's heart felt as though it was going to burst right out of her chest, as she followed the policemen down the steps.

What should she do? Call out? Warn Paul? Before he led the police right to Melissa's body? What else could he be doing there in the middle of the night? Was it possible he was looking for something else? Some other piece of evidence he'd remembered. Something which would put him in the clear?

Or was he just wandering? Sleepwalking? Did he even know where he was? What did he possibly think he could find blundering about in the total darkness of the bushes?

'Paul!'

She couldn't help it. She called out and the older of the two policemen immediately switched on a torch to reveal a figure running away from them.

'Paul!' Laura called out again, as Carl pushed past her. 'Paul, wait!'

A moment's hesitation was enough to slow him down, to allow Carl to catch up.

'Let me go! Let me go!' Paul shouted, as Carl grabbed hold of him.

'It's OK,' said Carl. 'It's OK. I'm not going to hurt you. But I don't want you to hurt yourself either, right? So just stand still and I'll let go, OK?'

'You can't stop me,' said Paul, trying to pull free. 'I have to go. I have to.'

'Go where?' said Laura, catching up with them, pushing Carl out of the way, grabbing hold of Paul's hands.

'I don't know,' said Paul, his eyes wide and frightened in the glare of the torch. 'I don't know. She's here. She's back. I have to find her.'

He whirled round to the right, lifting Laura's arm with his as he pointed.

'The café?' said the older policeman, who'd been standing some way back, muttering into a phone or radio link. 'Is that where you're heading? The café's through there.'

'The café?' Laura repeated

She knew it, of course. Everyone did. It had been closed for over ten years. In those ten years it had been the haunt of kids, vagrants, winos, druggies. It had been sealed up, vandalised and resealed. There had been talk of pulling it down. Then talk of clearing the undergrowth, opening the café up again, making it part of the revival of their town which somehow never happened.

And it had been one of the first places the police searched when Paul and Melissa had gone missing. In the dark, Laura had completely lost track of her bearings and had no idea which direction the café was in but Paul seemed quite definite about where he wanted to go and was pulling away from her.

'We have to get you back,' she told him. 'You're freezing. I'm freezing. We can look in the morning. Or let the police look. Let me take you back. Come on, Paul.'

'No!' he screamed, pulling away from her and kicking out at Carl, who tried to restrain him.

'All right,' said the older policeman, thrusting the torch into Laura's hand and grabbing hold of Paul himself. 'All right. It isn't far. We'll take a look if that's what you want to do. Just calm down.'

'It might be best,' Carl said, as Laura protested. 'Just let him see what he wants to see, then we'll coax him back.'

'There won't be anything to see,' said Laura.

'I know there won't,' said Carl. 'I was part of the team who searched the area. But just let him look, OK? Now keep the torch up, like that. Watch those brambles.'

Carl unhooked a bare, thorny branch from her jacket and guided her forward.

'Get that torch here quick,' the other policeman shouted.

Laura stumbled on to see him and Paul standing by the doorway of the café. Part of the roof was missing. The windows were boarded. But the door was half open, swinging and creaking.

'We broke it when we looked before,' said Carl, taking the torch from Laura, moving forward.

All four of them crowded round the doorway, as Carl shone the torch inside. A quick sweep, at first. The action of someone who expected to see nothing unusual. Then a slower arm movement, directing the beam onto the dusty floor. Onto the shape stretched out there, lying amongst the bottles, cans, cartons and other debris.

Laura heard herself scream as Paul darted forward and knelt by the still figure of Melissa.

Chapter 16

Laura screamed again as the dead body suddenly raised its head, hands going up to cover the face. Against the glare of the torch? Or to hide the scars?

'I'm cold,' said Melissa.

'What have they done?' Paul was asking. 'Melissa, what have they done to you?'

'I want to go home,' said Melissa. 'I was so cold and so frightened. Take me home.'

Laura backed out, leant against the outside of the building and tried to breathe deeply. The stench from that room was almost as overpowering as the shock. Sweat, sickness, urine, debris and dust which still caught in her throat, making her retch as the sound of hurrying footsteps and the flicker of torches came towards her. First the paramedics with a stretcher, then Laura's dad, then Melissa's parents, pushing past everyone screaming and shouting.

In the frenzied activity which followed Laura found it hard to focus on anything but the single fact. Melissa was alive. Against all hope, all reason, they had found her alive. That, for the moment, was enough.

The hysteria from Melissa's parents barely registered. Nor did Paul's new repetitive statement.

'It doesn't make sense. It doesn't make sense.'

A statement he was still making the following afternoon as he paced up and down his hospital room, with Laura anxiously watching.

'Paul, please sit down,' Laura said. 'The doctor said you should rest and besides, you're making me dizzy with all this pacing.'

'OK, I'll sit,' said Paul, flopping down on the bed, next to Laura. 'But it won't make any difference. How am I supposed to rest? You've heard what she's been saying. It's not true. It doesn't make any sense.'

'It makes a lot more sense than what you've been gibbering recently,' said Laura, trying to smile, trying to lighten things. 'I mean maybe it's not what you remember. Maybe it's not what you want to remember. Hardly surprising after what she made you do.'

'Don't start, Laura,' Paul shouted. 'Don't start piling all the blame on Melissa.'

'I'm not,' said Laura. 'I'm not blaming anybody. I'm only repeating what Melissa's told the doctors and police herself.'

'She's lying,' said Paul.

'Look,' said Laura. 'Even if her story isn't a hundred per cent true...'

'It's not even one per cent true.'

'Let's not quibble about statistics...let's just work through what she said. She'd been pushing you for ages to help her get some pills and stuff, right?'

'Right.'

'And you wouldn't?'

'Dead right.'

'But eventually she persuaded you?'

'No!'

'She got the stuff herself then, like she said?'

'Yes. But we never touched it. She didn't take it.'

'Melissa's taking full responsibility, Paul,' said Laura gently. 'Even if you admit to it, there won't be any charges. Melissa's insisting that she was to blame. That she forced you into it.'

'I'm not admitting it because it isn't true.'

'OK ... Let's try again. You go on your usual nightly ramble on Saturday night?'

Paul nodded.

'And Melissa shows you a bag of bottles ... pills, booze?'

'She showed me, yes. But that's as far as it got.'

'Whisky, vodka, water, pills,' Laura added. 'All the bottles they found in the bushes and around the old café. All empty.'

'Which could have belonged to anyone,' said Paul. 'You know the type who hang round there. And what about the next bit, Laura? Does this make sense? Melissa's saying that not only did I let her take the stuff but I took it myself! I know you all think I'm crazy but I'm not as crazy as that. I'm not even crazy enough to let Melissa do it. Suicide pact? Does that sound true to you, Laura? Or does it sound like a typical Melissa melodrama?'

'Both,' said Laura. 'I can imagine how desperate Melissa was. How she would have done anything to get her way. How influenced you always were by Melissa. How she could have talked you into it.'

'Melissa might have had me wrapped round her little finger, as you were so fond of saying but get this . . . no one but no one could have talked me into trying to kill myself. Why would I do that, Laura? Why?'

'I don't know,' Laura confessed. 'Melissa's saying . . .'

She paused. No one had told Paul this bit yet.

'Come on, Laura. Spit it out. It can't be any worse than everything else she's been saying.'

'She says you felt guilty,' said Laura hurriedly. 'She says you told her that you once wished her dead . . . that you had a sort of premonition. About the motorbike accident. That you somehow believed you made it happen. Oh, I know that bit can't be true. I know she's lying about that. I know you could never have thought anything like that, Paul, but . . .'

Trust Laura not to believe the only thing in Melissa's story which was true, Paul thought.

'Even if it was true,' Paul managed to say. 'I still wouldn't have tried to kill myself! I wouldn't have . . .'

'Wouldn't you, Paul?' said Laura gently. 'I don't know how she did it, but if Melissa had, somehow, made you feel responsible, guilty, isn't it possible that you might have done what she asked? And isn't it possible,' she added, hurriedly, before he could protest, 'that you'd later try to block out what you'd done. Especially with all that muck sloshing about in your system?'

'With all that muck,' Paul said. 'With all the stuff

146

Melissa says we swallowed, why aren't we dead? You'd have thought at least one of us would have succeeded, wouldn't you? I mean Melissa's wasn't exactly in peak condition to start with. How come we survived?'

'You puked most of it up, Melissa says . . . Or at least she did. Then she panicked. Trying to kill herself was one thing. Seeing you lying next to her, unconscious, was another. She managed to crawl over to you. Rammed her fingers down your throat. Made you puke up too.'

'And with all this drama and vomiting going on, nobody found us? Not one of the scores of people who were out there searching saw or heard anything?'

'Melissa can't explain that.'

'You don't say!'

'But it happens sometimes. Search parties miss things. Melissa says you were hidden well away. That you must have both lost consciousness again. That when you came round, you managed to carry Melissa to the shelter of the café . . . after it had been searched. When the door had already been broken open. That you eventually went off to get help.'

'So,' said Paul. 'If it was so straightforward, why didn't I get help? Why did I keep saying "it didn't happen"?'

'You had a breakdown, Paul,' said Laura. 'I didn't ever want to believe that but it's true. The strain, the guilt, the fear, all the stuff you'd taken. It's hardly surprising. But you came round. You forced yourself round in time to remember where you'd left her. In time to find her alive.'

'Regular hero, then, aren't I?' said Paul. 'No wonder

147

you want to believe her, for once. But there's just one tiny problem. It isn't true.'

'Then what is? What's your explanation?'

'She chose to come back,' said Paul. 'Because of me. She let them reverse the work they'd done! Send her back, paralysed and scarred. But she didn't have to do that. She was well again. She was beautiful.'

'Dreams, Paul,' said Laura, trying not to cry. 'Drug and alcohol-induced dreams and hallucinations. The colours you described, the detached voices, the heightened senses, the euphoria . . . they're all classic drug symptoms. You twisted them in your mind. Saw what you wanted to see. Believed what you wanted to believe. There were no aliens, Paul. No magical cures. Melissa will have to do it the hard way. Step by step. I think she understands that now. And if she does, then maybe some good has come out of this mess. Maybe having tried death, she'll realise that it's better to be alive. However hard life seems.'

'Don't!' said Paul. 'Don't spout all that moral claptrap at me. This is Melissa we're talking about. She'll never cope like that, never! I gave her a chance. They gave her a chance. A chance to be better again. And she didn't take it. She came back. Why would she do that? She didn't have to do that. I've got to see her. I've got to see her.'

'Paul,' said Laura firmly. 'They're not going to let you near anyone, let alone Melissa, if you carry on talking like that. They're going to lock you up and throw away the key . . . I'm sorry. I didn't mean it. The dreams, the hallucinations will pass. Dr Kapra said so. But you've got to try, Paul. Think it out, rationally. Try to face up to what really happened. And if you can't, just yet, then for heaven's sake, pretend. You won't do yourself or anyone else any good with all this talk of aliens. And you certainly won't help Melissa. She's got to come to terms with reality too.'

'I know,' said Paul. 'It's just that my reality's sort of different from everyone else's. And I can't make anyone understand. I can't make them believe me. Not even you.'

'No you can't, Paul,' said Laura shaking her head. 'Not even me. I've tried. I've really tried. And when Melissa was still missing, I was halfway there. Even aliens were better than believing you harmed her. But there were no aliens, Paul. Not ever. It was a fantasy which settled in your head when you fell off your bike that time and later re-surfaced with all the trauma of Melissa's accident and the pressure she was putting you under. And, in time, you'll come to see it as that too. But, for now...'

'For now I pretend?' said Paul. 'I go along with Melissa's story.'

'It's best,' said Laura. 'Believe me it's best.'

Chapter 17

PAUL

Even when I started going along with the story, telling them what they wanted to hear, I wasn't allowed to see Melissa. She was weak, traumatised. Undergoing tests. Not well enough for visitors.

So it was more than a week after we found her, that I finally got to talk to her and only then because she was insisting on seeing me. I'd been let out of hospital, on the understanding that I'd have a weekly visit to a counsellor. And it was after the first of my sessions that I went up to the ward to see Melissa.

'Paul!' she screamed, throwing her arms open wide, closing them round me as I sat down on the bed beside her. 'Paul, I'm so sorry.'

Sorry? What did she have to be sorry about? I was fine. But Melissa! It was all I could do to stop myself crying as I eased myself out of her grip and looked at her.

'You can go,' she informed her mother who'd been hovering over us. 'I want to talk to Paul on my own.'

'I don't think...' Melissa's mother began.

'I said go!' Melissa yelled.

Mrs Kingsley-Porter went, closing the door behind her, following Melissa's screamed instruction.

'I'm sorry,' Melissa said again. 'Are you OK? Really OK? They said you were but I couldn't be sure. I could have killed you with my selfish stupidity. I could have killed us both.'

She looked towards the door as she spoke as if she was scared someone was lurking outside, listening.

'It's OK,' I said. 'There's no one around. We can talk now. About what really happened.'

'I've told them what really happened,' she said. 'I've told them everything. They know it wasn't your fault. They know I pushed you into it.'

'Not that,' I whispered. 'I know what you've said and I've backed your story up. Every word. It's best that way. But we're on our own now. We can talk. What happened, Melissa? Why did you do it? Why did you come back? You didn't have to do that. I would have managed. I would have been OK. I could have made them believe me, in the end.'

'I knew it,' said Melissa suddenly starting to cry. 'I knew you weren't really well. I knew you weren't really better. That's why I wanted to see for myself.'

'What do you mean?' I said.

'The hallucinations,' she said, sniffing and reaching for a tissue from the bedside table. 'The aliens. Mum told me what you'd been saying. Before they found me. And I knew what had happened. The tablets, the whisky and stuff had made the hallucinations worse.'

'They're not hallucinations,' I insisted. 'Don't you remember? Don't you remember Krespron and Torflin?

Don't you remember being well again? Don't you remember bouncing up and down on the gel cushion?'

'All I remember,' said Melissa. 'Is waking up, almost choking on my own vomit. Seeing you lying there, next to me. Thinking you were dead! Thinking, oh my God, what have I done? Shaking you. Scratching at you. Hitting you across the face. Using energy I didn't even know I had anymore. Pounding your chest with my fists. Maybe that's the bouncing up and down, you remember. I don't know. But when I finally got you round to some sort of consciousness, you were rambling about an octopus and then you started on about aliens under the sea. And even after we'd both come round a bit, even after you dragged me to the shelter of the café, you still seemed to be in some other reality. Telling me that the disgusting things scurrying over me weren't spiders! Telling me they were going to make me better. And then, you collapsed again, exhausted. I think we both did. I don't know how long we were out for. But when I woke up, you were sitting on the floor, talking to someone.'

'Who?' I said. 'What did they look like?'

'How should I know?' said Melissa. 'It wasn't a real someone. There was no one there. You were talking to empty space. Saying you were going home but I'd have to stay. Which sort of made sense as you can walk and I can't. So I told you to go and get help. And I should have known. I should have known you weren't... weren't quite well... Because, as you were leaving, you stopped at the door. Said goodbye. Told me they'd look after me. And there were tears in your eyes. Like it was final. And I began to think you wouldn't come back. That I'd die there, on my own. And I started screaming, crying, throwing things but nobody heard. And I was so scared, Paul . . .'

The terror was in her eyes, as she spoke. No act this. She believed what she was saying, she really believed it. Implanted memories? Or was it true? Was Melissa's reality right and mine wrong?

I had one more try.

'Just listen to me,' I said. 'Just let me try to explain one thing. It's important you know this even if you never believe it.'

'Is it about aliens?' she said.

'Yes but if you listen to this I promise I won't mention them ever again.'

'OK,' she said. 'Deal.'

'I think what you're seeing are implanted memories . . . In my reality, in my memory, we really did make contact with aliens. You don't need to know the details but what I want you to know, what I want you to understand, is that they made you well. Totally well.'

She smiled as I described it all. As if, for a minute, she was really with me. Really seeing. Really believing.

'Yeah,' she said, at one point. 'Sounds like me. Given a choice of being well with the aliens or grotesque back here, I'd have stayed. No contest.'

'But you didn't,' I said. 'And that's what I wanted you to know. You made the choice, Melissa. You chose to come back. To protect me. Because I was getting in a

153

mess. Because I could never have explained. Because I'd have ended up in a prison or a loony bin.'

She started to laugh. The old Melissa fun-filled shriek.

'Well that sort of proves it's fantasyland, doesn't it?' she said. 'Octopus surgeons, I could just about believe. Gel clouds and amphibious spaceships, OK. But me doing something altruistic? Choosing to come back because of you or anyone else. Get real, Paul. This is me, you're talking about. Surely even you can see it's fantasy? I'm not like that, Paul. Never have been, never will be. Only in your imagination, sunshine. But thanks . . .'

She squeezed my hand.

'It's nice to know I'm a heroine, even if it's only in someone's dreams. Hey,' she said, still smiling. 'You could cash in on these dreams of yours. They'd make a great film. Directed by Paul Crompton. Starring Melissa Kingsley-Porter as the heroine who returns from her watery heaven to save the boy she loves. What do you think? If they ever patch me up well enough to get to drama school . . . we'd make a great team.'

There were just a few flaws in her plans, of course. Not least the fact that I've got no ambitions to be a film director. I'm torn, at the moment, between becoming a marine zoologist or an astronomer. Because one day, somehow, I'm going to prove that there are other intelligent life forms out there in the galaxy or even amongst us, here. I'm going to prove it to other people. Prove it to myself. Prove that I'm not mad. Wasn't ever mad. Wasn't drugged up. Suicidal. Crazy. Not even slightly delusional.

Trouble is, I'm going to need some seriously good qualifications for either of those careers and I haven't exactly made a stunning start. Even with the counselling, it took me ages to get the scrambled mess that was my brain back into any sort of order. Months and months. And, by the time I did, it was too late for GCSEs. I'd missed a lot of the coursework deadlines and didn't even bother to sit the exams.

Laura reckons I did it on purpose. So I could repeat Year 11, with Melissa. But that's Laura spouting gibberish, as usual. I didn't even know Melissa was going to come back to school at all until last week. I don't think she knew herself.

It was the last lot of plastic surgery which swung it. Melissa's looking pretty good now. Not perfect but the surgeons were amazed at how well the skin responded to the grafts.

She's still in her wheelchair but recently she's taken a few steps using a walking frame. The chair she's got now is motorised. Really flash. And it makes it easier for her to get out and about on her own, which she does, stopping to tell anyone who'll listen that she's determined to get better. Showing them the little album of photographs she's putting together, monitoring her progress. And, in pride of place, at the front, are the computer generated images of how she'll look when all the treatment's finished.

'Typical Melissa,' Laura said. 'Never does anything by halves.'

155

And I suppose she's right. Melissa's made the switch from suicidal tragedy queen to battling warrior princess brilliantly. Oh, she still has her depressions but most of the time she's happy enough, I guess. Back in the limelight. Being the centre of attention. Where Melissa will always belong.

Most believe that her attempt to overdose, her close encounter with death, brought about the change. What I call 'the Laura theory'.

Me? Well I'm thinking close encounters of another sort and I can't help remembering something the aliens said, when they talked about reversing the operation, sending Melissa home.

'You won't feel pain, Melissa, and if it is possible to make minor repairs to make you more comfortable, without being so noticeable, then we will authorise it. We are not cruel. We do not wish you to suffer.'

And I like to think that they didn't fully reverse the operation. Or that they did something that would allow Melissa's body to respond to treatment better, or allow her mind to think more positively. Perhaps all three.

And I know that one day, I'll come across them again. Maybe everyone will. Maybe my aliens will make proper contact. When the time is right.

Only I keep my thoughts to myself. Because part of me, the sane part, the part that listens to Laura, my parents, the doctors and Melissa, knows it can't be true.

It didn't happen.